George John Whyte-Melville

Roy's Wife

A Novel: Vol. I.

George John Whyte-Melville

Roy's Wife
A Novel: Vol. I.

ISBN/EAN: 9783337045012

Printed in Europe, USA, Canada, Australia, Japan

Cover: Foto ©Andreas Hilbeck / pixelio.de

More available books at **www.hansebooks.com**

ROY'S WIFE.

VOL. I.

ROY'S WIFE

A Novel.

BY

G. J. WHYTE-MELVILLE.

IN TWO VOLUMES.

VOL. I.

LONDON:

CHAPMAN AND HALL, 193 PICCADILLY

1878.

Bungay:

CLAY AND TAYLOR, PRINTERS.

CONTENTS OF VOL. I.

CHAP.		PAGE
I.	A PINT OF PORT	1
II.	A PAIR OF BOOTS	22
III.	NO. 46	30
IV.	DEEPER AND DEEPER	44
V.	A WOMAN'S REASON	56
VI.	SO LIKE A MAN!	69
VII.	WARDEN TOWERS	83
VIII.	ROYSTON GRANGE	97
IX.	STRANGERS YET	113
X.	MRS. MOPUS	125
XI.	A WALKING DICTIONARY	139
XII.	BURTON BRAKE	155

CHAP.

XIII. SWEET SYMPATHY ... ..

XIV. SO FAR AWAY ... ..

XV. THE LITTLE RIFT ... ..

XVI. THE MUSIC MUTE ...

XVII. BAFFLED ... .

XVIII. DO YOU REMEMBER? ..

XIX. IN THE WILDERNESS ..

XX. A BLUE-JACKET ... ..

ROY'S WIFE.

CHAPTER I.

A PINT OF PORT.

NONE of your Scotch pints, dear to hard-headed North Britons of the last century, not even an imperial pint, containing only one-fourth of the former measure, but an hotel pint, in hotel limits, of hotel vintage, at hotel price. Sound, no doubt, though rough and fruity; strong, full-flavoured, and exceedingly restorative to body and mind.

An open wine-book propped against an uncorked bottle offers the produce of many European vineyards at the highest possible tariff. In its first page alone the varieties of

champagne and claret might stock the cellar of
a duke. But he is a man of unusually trustful
nature who drinks wine in a coffee-room at
the rate of one hundred and twenty shillings
per dozen, and experienced travellers wisely
content themselves with pale ale, brandy-and-
water, a glass of brown sherry, or a pint of
port.

Neither wine nor wine-card have yet
attracted attention from the visitor who
ordered both. A waiter, banging hot plates
down under his nose, to serve "a bit of fish,"
notices nothing remarkable in this unit among
many guests. His manners are quiet, he wears
a good coat, and drinks wine with his dinner ;
the waiter, therefore, considers him a gentleman. That his face should be weary, his air
abstracted, seems but the natural result of a
journey by rail from London to the seaside ;
and if he thinks of him at all, it is as "a gent
from town," good for a shilling or two when
he takes his departure, notwithstanding that
"attendance " is charged in the bill.

The fish has been to London and back since leaving its native shore, and is sent away uneaten; but the port is sipped, tasted, and approved. The first glass permeates through his tired frame till it tingles at his finger-ends; with the second, there rises a sensation of renewed vigour and vitality in the whole man; ere he is half-way to the bottom of the third, a change has come over himself, his surroundings, his past, his present—above all, his future—that future which looked so blank and uninteresting ten minutes ago. The carpet seems no longer faded, the coffee-room dingy and ill-ventilated. A stout lady at the corner table, dining in solemn silence with two shy daughters and an ungainly son, ceases to be an object of aversion and disgust. Even the old gentleman by the window, who gasps and snorts during the process of deglutition, now excites no stronger feeling than a mild hope that he will presently be seized with some kind of fit, such as shall necessitate his removal up-stairs. The drinker is surprised at his own

benevolence, and wonders, not without contempt, how such an alteration should have been
wrought in his nature by warmth, food, and a
pint of port !

Reflection has been forced on him in the
contrast between present inactivity and the
stir of his former life. With nothing to do,
plenty of time to do it, and nobody to help
him, he has become a philosopher in spite of
himself. He has acquired the habit of analyzing
his own character and motives, examining them,
as it were, from an outside point of view, in a
spirit of cynicism, half-scornful, half-indulgent,
but wholly without result, his speculations only
leading him farther and farther into that
labyrinth of which *cui bono* is the centre and
the goal. He is easily depressed : no wonder.
But his hopes rise quickly as they fall. When
he sat down to dinner he felt a hundred years
old, yet ere the most odorous of Cheddar
cheeses can be thrust in his face, the world we
live in has acquired a new lustre, a fresh
interest; society seems no longer an infliction

nor life a mistake. It is his nature to accept
the metamorphosis with amusement, curiosity,
and mistrust. "What an absurdity," he
reflects, "is this action and reaction of body
and mind, this irregular and spontaneous
oscillation that governs the machine called
man—a machine in some respects constructed
with such elaborate care and precision, in
others lamentably ill-suited to the purposes of
life! A steam-engine is not thrown out of
gear because we feed its fires with inferior
coal, or lubricate its hinges with a cheaper oil
than the best by sixpence a gallon; but the
man who invented the steam-engine can be
driven into madness in three minutes with as
many glasses of brandy, and only half-a-pound
of such a cheese as that, for instance, would
weigh him down with a depression wanting
but a few grains of actual despair. If the
master-piece of nature, the lord of creation,
had been made with a gizzard, rather than a
liver, would he not oftener be lord of himself?
which is more to the purpose; and would not

that self more seldom prove 'a heritage of woe'? I have sat here but five-and-twenty minutes by the coffee-room clock. The waiter thinks I am the same person whose orders he took for dinner, and who told him to remove the fish *at once.* How little he knows! That man and I are as different as chalk itself from the very cheese that still pervades the room. He was a pessimist—almost a devil-worshipper; I am an optimist, and in so far a good Christian that I am at peace with all mankind! When I drew my chair to this table I felt, to use the expression of an Irish friend, as if 'the back-bone was out of me.' No interest, no energy, no concern for my luggage, no British susceptibility to imposition, scarcely enough spirit available to have resented an insult or returned a blow. Now I have become curious about the locality, the neighbourhood, the shops, the church, the circulating library, the new pier, and the state of the tide. I ascertain by personal inquiry that my portmanteau is safe in No. 5. I cannot be overcharged at present,

inasmuch as I have scarcely yet laid the foundation of a bill, but I am prepared to expend
guineas rather than be cheated out of shillings;
while as for blows and insults, my arm has kept
my head ere now. Let the aggressor look out;
I am well able to take care of myself. And
all this has been brought about by the consumption of a pint of port. Great heavens!
can it be possible that my intellect, my sagacity,
my nobler qualities, even my courage, are thus
dependent on drink! Life was a very dull
business half-an-hour ago. The journey, though
smooth and easy, had become so slow and tiresome; the road was exceedingly uninteresting,
leading nowhere in particular after all. For
me and for my neighbours the way made, like
that of an unskilful swimmer, was so out of
proportion to the energy expended, the puffing
and blowing, the hurry, the effort, and the
splash! We were all, like flies on a window-
pane, buzzing to and fro, backwards and for-
wards, round and round, never relaxing our
efforts, yet never penetrating an impassable

transparency that kept us from the reality outside. I have envied a man breaking stones on the road, because with a daily duty and a definite purpose he seemed in some measure to fulfil the object of existence, and to be less of a sham and mountebank than myself. I am satisfied now that such reflections were but results of a languid circulation. My pulse—for I felt it when the waiter wasn't looking—beats full and regular, seventy to the minute; I seem still to have duties, pleasures, perhaps even happiness, in store for one whose scalp is not yet bare, and who can count the grey hairs in his whiskers. Waiter, a toothpick!"

"Beg your pardon, sir; we don't keep them in the coffee-room now, sir."

"Indeed! Why not?"

"We found it didn't answer, sir. The gentlemen took them away."

Lost in the field of reflection opened up by such an admission, our visitor might have relapsed into something of his previous despondency, but that his attention was

diverted to the laying of a table at the other
end of the room with rather more preparation
and nicety of arrangement than had been
accorded in his own case, though his sense of
smell caused him to suspect that the fish he
had discarded was brought to the front once
more. Spoons and forks, however, had been
polished to a dazzling lustre, the tablecloth was
very white, and in its centre stood a handful
of flowers in a dull glass vase. Surveying this
effort, the waiter smiled satisfaction, while our
philosopher threw himself back in his chair
to see what would come of it with the good-
humoured indifference of a man who has dined.

What came of it was nothing unusual to
the waiter, to the old gentleman, to the mother
and daughters, even to the ungainly son—
simply a single lady dining later than other
inmates of the hotel; but to the port-drinker,
in regular gradations, at a startling rate of
progression, a distraction, an amusement, a
mystery, an engrossing interest, and an irresistible attraction.

The very rustle of her dress, as it swept the dingy coffee-room carpet, was suggestive of grace and dignity, of a smooth, easy gait, springing from symmetry of form and vigorous elasticity of limb. That horses can go in all shapes is an established maxim of the stable, but when women are good movers it needs no anatomist to assure us that in external structure at least they have been "nobly planned." Even the waiter seemed impressed, smirking and flourishing his napkin with unusual emphasis, while interposing his person between the object of his assiduities and the observer who wanted to see her face. It vexed him that this should be completely averted. As the lady seated herself, he could only detect the turn of a full and shapely figure, a delicate little ear, and a white neck from which the hair was scrupulously lifted and arranged, dark and lustrous, tight and trim, in a fashion exceedingly becoming to the beautiful, but trying to the more ordinary of womankind.

Many a romance has been built on slighter

scaffolding; and no young man of half his age and a quarter his experience was more likely to make a fool of himself about a woman than the gentleman in question—John Roy, Esquire, of Royston, a deputy-lieutenant for his county, and a magistrate who had never qualified in the Commission of the Peace. There was nothing uncommon in his history. Eton and the ten-oar — Oxford and the drag — upper division, fifth form, at school, and a degree at college—woodcocks in Albania, lansqueret at St. Petersburg, Hanover for German, Paris for fencing, and home again for real enjoyment of life—then a little Melton, a little Newmarket, a little London, with the prospect of completing this conventional course in a prudent marriage, and such rural vegetation as would tend to the increase of personal weight and prolongation of the family tree.

Not the best training, perhaps, even for the level path he seemed ·likely to tread in the journey of life. Not the wisest preparation, certainly, for a time when there must be an end of business and pleasure; when tobacco shall cease to soothe, and wine to exhilarate; when dancing waters and June sunshine are to be exchanged for drawn curtains and beef-tea; when it will need neither the doctor's grave face nor the nurse's vapid smile to tell us that we have done with our accustomed habits, pursuits, and interests; never to greet our guests, ride our horses, nor balance our accounts again; no more to cherish a grudge, nor indulge a prejudice, nor kindle in the glow of a kindly action on behalf of our fellow-man! The journey is compulsory, the destination inevitable, yet how little thought we seem to take for here or hereafter!

In Eastern nations every male, whatever may be his rank, is brought up to some kind of handicraft, and so far is made independent of external fortune. In England, we pride ourselves on teaching our sons a smattering of many things, and a thorough knowledge of none. This we call the education of a gentleman; but surely, in such loose, discursive culture of the mind, we fail to stimulate that power of concentration which can alone remove gigantic obstacles, to encourage that habit of persistency which forms the very back-bone of success.

John Roy received "the education of a gentleman," and did credit to his nurture as well as another; but there came a time, before he was turned thirty, when he wished he had been bred a shoemaker, or a stonemason, because of the dull dead pain for which there is no anodyne like the pressure of daily want and the fatigue of daily work.

The lives of most of us in so far resemble a skein of silk, that they unwind freely and readily enough until they arrive at a knot. Patient, even pleased, we sit in a ludicrous attitude, stiffened by the voluntary fetters that a pair of white hands have fitted deftly round our wrists, and while we smile and look foolish, lo! there is a jerk, a quiver, a stop : the pretty lips tighten, the pencilled eyebrows frown, and presently the merry-go-round that went so swimmingly comes to a dead-lock. So she brings out her scissors to solve the whole difficulty with a vicious little snip, observing calmly, "I began at the wrong end."

There was a Lady Jane in Roy's life who also began at the wrong end. She chose to fall in love with him because she was idle, because her younger sister was engaged, because he always stood at the same place in the park when she rode there, perhaps because the London season is so insufferably tedious without some definite attraction. Having decided that she would "like him a little," she made up her mind that he should like her a great deal. There was no difficulty in the capture. Handsome and high-bred, asked everywhere, and sufficiently admired even in London, she had but to look her wishes; in three days the man was at her beck and call. Such stories have been told so often they are hardly worth repeating. He had never really cared for a woman before, he never cared quite in the same way for a woman again.

Men, like animals, take their punishment differently according to their dispositions. Some fret and chafe, and forget all about it; others turn cowardly and despondent, or sullen and savage, but all lose something of that fire and dash which prompts untried natures to achieve the marvellous in aiming at the impossible.

Lady Jane, with her new distraction, was very happy for a fortnight, a month, six weeks! It seemed so nice to be petted, to be worshipped, to have some twelve stone of manhood all to oneself. She felt quite sorry for the other girls, plodding along, dismounted as it were, while she rode her hobby in triumph with her delicate nose in the air. Mr. Roy— she wished he had a prettier name than John— was so devoted, so amiable, above all so true. He never gave her the slightest twinge of jealousy (she would have liked him all the better if he had), but told her every hour that she was too good for him; a princess stooping to a squire, Beauty smiling on the Beast, and

that he considered himself unworthy to wipe
the very dust from her feet. After a while
she believed him, as a woman will believe
anything, if it is only repeated often enough;
and when she overheard Aunt Julia whisper
to mamma that "Jane might do so much
better," began to think perhaps Aunt Julia
was right.

"She stopped it before they were regularly engaged. Nobody could accuse Jane of
behaving badly,"—so said her family,—"and
if Mr. Roy had presumed on the high spirits
and fascinating manners of a girl who was
popular with everybody, he might thank his
own folly for his disappointment."

They allowed, however, that he "behaved
beautifully," as did Jane, who returned everything he had given her, except some music;
and on the one occasion when they met in
society after their rupture, shook hands with
him as kindly and calmly as if he had been her
grandfather.

He saw a fresh admirer, with a large rent-

roll, put his arm round her waist for a waltz,
and stepped into the street with a strange
numb feeling, like a patient whose leg has
been cut off—the sensation was akin to relief,
yet in some respects, worse to bear than pain.
It was characteristic of the man that he never
blamed her. " I suppose they are all alike,"
he said to his cigar, and so, walking home in
the rain, made up his mind that this also was
vanity !

Lady Jane rode in the park pretty regularly
till the end of the season, sometimes with,
sometimes without, the eligible admirer; but
she looked in vain for Mr. Roy's figure at the
accustomed spot; missing it none the less,
perhaps, that she wondered what had become
of him, and whether he did not sometimes
think of her still ?

John Roy was the last man to howl.
Nobody else should know how hard he was hit.
His stronger nature told him that he was
meant for something better than to be the
puppet of a woman's smile, and, though they

smarted intolerably, he had the grace to be
ashamed of his wounds. By the time Lady
Jane went to Cowes, he was whirling a lasso
at wild horses in South America, living on
beef and water, burning quantities of tobacco,
and spending sixteen hours out of the four-
and-twenty on a Mexican saddle in the open
air. Smoking and riding combined, soon
modified the symptoms of his malady; its
cure, though slow, was progressive. In twelve
months he felt resigned, and in eighteen,
comfortable. After two or three years he
came back to Europe, having travelled over a
great part of the world, with nothing left to
remind him of his pangs but a cynical resolve
never to be caught in such a trap again.
"Not if I know it!" says he who has once
burned his fingers; but the spark kindles
when he does *not* know it, and the flame
consumes him none the less greedily, that he
has been dried and seasoned in the heat of a
former fire.

Royston was got ready for its owner; but

he only lived there at intervals, trying to do his duty as a landlord for a time, then flying off at a tangent to seek some distraction, in however mild a change, from the weariness of his every-day life.

Thus it was that a September evening found him in a quiet watering-place on the southern coast, speculating, after a coffee-room dinner, on the beauty of features and sweetness of disposition suggested by the back of a lady's head. Watch as he would, she never turned it so much as an inch. There was the beautiful ear, the white skin, the trim, dark hair, but nothing more. How if the rest of her person should in no way correspond with this exquisite sample? She might squint, she might have lost her teeth, she might wear a wooden leg! He had heard or read of such disillusions, such disappointments. The uncertainty began to get irksome, annoying, intolerable. Could he not make some excuse to walk across the room yonder, to the chimney-piece, where he would be full in front of her? To look at the clock,

for instance; the dial of that time-piece being
a foot in diameter, and calculated for short-
sighted inquirers at ten paces off. He had
already moved his chair, when she rose.
"Forty-six, if you please," she said to the
waiter in a low, sweet voice, as indicating the
number of her apartment, for proper registry
of her bill, and so walked smoothly and
gracefully to the door.

Disappointment! disillusion! Not a bit of
it! As lovely a face as a man could wish to
look at, set on as shapely a form! Features
not quite classical, only because so soft and
womanly; deep grey eyes, fringed with long
black lashes; a mouth too large, a chin too
prominent, but for the white teeth and perfect
curves of the one, the firm and well-cut outline
of the other. A complexion delicate rather
than pale, a figure somewhat full and tall, a
graceful head carried nobly on neck and
shoulders; last, not least, an abundance of
dark and silky hair, growing low on the brow,
square at the temples, and drawn tight off the

forehead to wind in thick shining coils round the skull.

Mr. Roy had a habit of talking to himself. "You darling!" he whispered, as the door closed. "That is the nicest woman I ever saw in my life!"

CHAPTER II.

A PAIR OF BOOTS.

THE smoke-room, as the waiter called it, was empty; our friend felt pleased to find that uncomfortable apartment at his sole disposal. Devoid of drapery, floored with oil-cloth, bare of all furniture but wooden chairs, horse-hair sofas, and spittoons; this retreat offered few temptations to a smoker, and such guests as were devoted to the practice usually chose to consume their tobacco out of doors. It was a bright night, with a clear sky and a rising tide, yet Roy seemed to prefer the flicker of gas in this dim, desolate apartment, to the fresh briny air and a moon-lit sea. To be under the same roof with her was a strong point; it would be his own fault if he could not, in some way, make the acquaintance of this fascinating

stranger before she left the hotel. He was a
man of the world, but he had seen a great deal
of that world with his own eyes, and travel,
no doubt, tends to simplify the character while
it enlarges the mind. He did not at once
suspect evil of her, because journeying unpro-
tected and alone; nor did he feel that so
attractive a woman must be in a false position,
without a companion of her own sex. Again
and again he rehearsed the little scene that he
hoped to bring about next day. The meeting
on the stairs, the profound and deferential bow,
repeated on the pier, so unobtrusively that to
offer a newspaper, a novel, a handful of fresh
flowers, would seem a tribute of homage rather
than an unauthorized impertinence; then, by
slow degrees, morning greetings, afternoon
conversations, perhaps at last a walk by the
sea, an explanation of motives, a hint at covert
admiration from the first, and so on—and so
on—to the end—

Here a memory of Lady Jane made him
catch his breath like the shock of a cold bath.

There was something of triumph, nevertheless, in the consciousness that he had hoisted the flag of freedom at last, and found, perhaps to-night by the merest accident, far more than he looked for in those young days of weakness, folly, and despair. How delightful it would be to instal her at Royston, to take her to London, to introduce her to Lady Jane? No. Already he had so far forgotten the ghost of his departed love, that he felt perfectly indifferent whether Lady Jane grudged him his happiness or not!

A man must marry some time, he decided. Would he ever see a woman so likely to suit him, supposing, of course, that she proved as charming as she looked? And why not? The face was surely an index to the character. Such soft and beautiful hair, too, must necessarily accompany an amiable disposition and well-stored mind. His thoughts were running away with him, galloping headlong down-hill, and had reached altar and honey-moon, when they were suddenly pulled up by a consideration that ought to have presented itself sooner. " What if she were married already?" How he cursed his stupidity not to have scrutinized her left hand for the plain gold ring that tells its respectable tale. Yes, of course, she must be married; that accounted for her travelling by herself, her quiet independence of manner, her dining alone in the coffee-room of an hotel. She came to meet her husband, who would, probably, arrive by the last train, and there was an end of the whole thing! As he dashed the stump of his cigar into the fireless grate, he could not help laughing aloud to think how quickly he had planned, built, furnished, and annihilated his castle in the air! Yet passing 46 in the passage on his way to bed he could not help looking wistfully at the closed door, with its painted numerals, wondering the while how he could be such a fool!

Roy was an early riser. The habit, acquired in warmer climates than our own, is got rid of with difficulty, even in England, where many

of us lose something like fourteen hours, or
one working day, in the week, by persistently
lying in bed till eight o'clock. On his dreams
it is needless to speculate; sleep does not
always continue the thread of our waking
thoughts, but he turned out at seven, and by
half-past was shaking the cold salt water from
eyes, ears, and nostrils, as he came up after a
glorious "header" and struck out for the
open sea.

He was a fair swimmer, but distances are
deceiving for a naked man in the Channel, so
that a few hundred yards out and in again
were as much as he cared to accomplish before
breakfast. Climbing into his machine, he
experienced that sensation of renewed vigour
in body and mind, which is never so delightful
as after the first of our morning dips, if we
are prudent enough not to stay in the sea too
long!

Walking home, through the market, with
a furious appetite for breakfast, all the
despondency of yesterday had vanished, and

even the infatuation of last night seemed but a dream.

Royston was no longer a dull and moated Grange, in which life meant stagnation; a country gentleman's duties and occupations assumed the importance which everything really possesses that is done heartily and for a good motive. John Roy himself had become an enviable person, with far better luck than he deserved; and this fresh, quiet Beachmouth a charming little watering-place where he would remain just long enough to enjoy his holiday, and return to homely duties refreshed, invigorated, altogether a new man. If No. 46 crossed his mind, it was only that he might picture her to himself eating prawns with her legal mate at a coffee-room breakfast, smiling and comely, no doubt, but not half so pretty as she looked the night before.

Proceeding upstairs to his own apartment he necessarily passed her door. On its threshold rested a dear little pair of boots, left out last night to be cleaned, and brought

back this morning, in company with a can of
warm water.   It was obvious they belonged to
a very pretty foot, slim and supple, hollow and
arched, that trod, light and even, on a thin
sole and a low heel.   For a man who admired
pretty feet it was impossible to pass these
boots without further examination.   John Roy
could not resist the temptation, and stooped to
pick one up.

Now the chambermaid, not wishing to go
more errands than necessary, had left a letter
for No. 46, cunningly balanced on that lady's
chaussure : was it quite inexcusable that Mr.
Roy should have turned it over in his hand,
or that his heart should have made a great
leap when he read the address—

"MISS BURTON,
                Imperial Hotel,
                        Beachmouth,"

written legibly enough in a plain, clerk-like,
current hand? Miss Burton! She was free
then, this goddess, unmarried at any rate,

though it would be too much to suppose that she could be without suitors. Still, give him a fair field and no favour, why should his chance be worse than another's? All the folly of last night, that he thought had been washed out by sea-water, came back with a rush; he lifted one of the little boots in a tender, almost a reverent hand; but for footsteps in the passage he would have defied blacking, and pressed it to his lips.

Instead of kissing, he dropped it like a hot potato, and hurried off to complete his toilet, with a light tread and a bounding pulse, but the fine appetite for breakfast completely gone.

CHAPTER III.

NO. 46.

HE was just in time. His own scarcely closed, before the door of 46 opened, and a bright, handsome face peeped out, followed by a round white arm, that drew letter, boots, and water-can into the room. Miss Burton then desisted from the sleeking of her dark locks, and proceeded to read the following communication :—

"Monday evening,
"Corner Hotel, Corner Street, Strand.

"MY DEAR NELLY,—

"You were disappointed. In course you must have been disappointed, though I make no account of disappointments myself, being well used to them. But you are young, which makes it different. Well, my dear, the

cabman was sulky, and his poor horse lame,
and I *had* very little time to spare, there's no
denying it, so we missed the train. Why
didn't I come by the next? I'll tell you.
The moment I got home, meaning to take a
cup of tea and a fresh start, what should I
find at the door, but four arrivals, and one of
them a family of eight, with a baby not short-
coated, bless it, as hungry as a little hawk.
Nothing ready, not so much as a mouthful of
toast for the lot. Maria is no more use than a
post; and when I think of how you would
have helped me, my dear, in such a muddle, I
could sit down and cry. Why, in *your* time, a
queen might have eaten off the kitchen floor,
and now, I declare, I am ashamed for the
strange servants to go into the offices. Even
them foreign couriers turn up their noses when
they pass in and out; and to be untidy, as
well you know, is the one thing that makes
me mad. However, I am such a one to bustle
when I'm really put to it, that I had them all
settled and comfortable before the gas was

turned on; but it was too late to start for
Beachmouth then. I never believed much in
telegraphs since the Government took them in
hand, so I thought I'd drop you a line by post,
my dear, to tell you all, how and about it.

"I made sure of being off first thing in
the morning, but we're poor blind creatures,
the sharpest of us, and half-an-hour back,
Fanny, that's the new under-housemaid, and a
precious lazy one she is, comes tapping at the
door, and 'If you please, ma'am,' says she,
'Miss Collins is took bad,' says she; and will
you believe it, my dear, there was Maria
fainted dead away on the stairs, and forced to
be put to bed at once, and a doctor sent for
and all! Till he has been, I don't know what's
the matter, nor how long a job it will be, nor
when I shall get down and join you, no more
than the dead. That's why I'm writing in
such a hurry to save the post, so please excuse
mistakes, and always believe me,

Your affectionate aunt,

Matilda Phipps."

"P.S. My head isn't worth twopence, I'm that worried and put about. Now I've forgot to say, you'd better keep your mind easy, and stay where you are,—the change will do you good. If things go well, I might be with you as Saturday, at soonest. I can tell you these fine autumn days make me long for a blow of the sea-breezes and a walk by the sea-side; good-bye."

After reading the above production more than once, Miss Burton pulled her purse from under the pillow, and counted her money, gold, silver, copper, and a bank-note. She then completed her toilet, took in a breakfast-tray left at the door, disposed of its contents with a healthy appetite, arranged her writing-case on the lid of a trunk, and, in a most uncomfortable attitude, produced the following reply :—

"Tuesday morning,
"No. 46, Imperial Hotel, Beachmouth.

"DEAR AUNT MATILDA,—

"Mind you ask for No. 46 when you arrive. It means *me.* I'm like a convict, only

without a brass ring, and the people of the
hotel wouldn't know me by any other name.
I hope you will be here soon; you *would* enjoy
it. From my window I have such a lovely
view of the sea, and this morning I was woke
by the tide coming in. It sounded so fresh
and healthy. I wonder anybody lives away
from the sea-side; not but what I was very
happy with you in Corner Street. I like to
think I am of use, and one is very useful, I
suppose, managing an hotel. If poor Miss
Collins keeps bad, I will come back whenever
you wish. I don't want to be independent,
dear auntie, and the money left me by Cousin
William I would willingly join to yours, if you
thought it a good plan, as I told you from the
first. However, in the mean time, we will
hope to enjoy ourselves for a fortnight at least,
in this beautiful and romantic place. Not that
I have seen much of it yet; but directly I
have posted this, I mean to be off for a long
walk by the sea. It seems like another world,
and yet I am sure I don't know why. This hotel

is comfortable enough, but I could teach them a
few things, I dare say, though to be sure we
Londoners are apt to expect too much. Country-
folks must be a little behindhand, I suppose.
How you would laugh if you were to find me
settled in the bar, taking the orders and posting
the books.   Wouldn't it seem like old times?

"I was glad you told me to travel first-
class, as I had a carriage all to myself, except
for two gentlemen, who got out half-way. I
never was much of a one to take notice of the
men, and though they stared more than was
polite, we scarcely exchanged a word. I dined
in the coffee-room, where there were very few
people. If it wasn't for the sea, I should be
dull enough; but I hope to have you here in
a day or two, when we will take some famous
walks, and perhaps, if it is very smooth, go
out for a sail. In the mean time I shall stay
where I am, dear auntie, till I hear from you
again, and remain always,

Your grateful and affectionate niece,

ELINOR BURTON."

Having stamped her letter, Miss Burton put on a killing little straw hat, armed herself with an umbrella, and sallied forth to the post-office, light of step and blithe of heart, little knowing, like the rest of us, what a day might bring forth.

It must not be supposed that this lady, though filling a social position no higher than the management of an hotel, owned and superintended by her aunt, was therefore deficient in education, or unrefined in feelings. Her father was a bookseller, her mother a governess. Such a combination inferred a moderate share of education and accomplishments. She could play the pianoforte, speak French, calculate figures, order dinner, see that it was properly cooked, check trades-people, manage servants, and wrote, moreover, the most beautiful Italian hand imaginable—clear, precise, and fluent, it seemed no unworthy index of her character.

She was now near thirty, and had of course received a fair amount of attention. She might have counted her offers as tumblers of punch are counted in Ireland, on the fingers of both hands. Hitherto she had escaped without a wound, almost without a scratch. Well-to-do tradesmen sued in vain. A rising artist, a popular actor were rejected, kindly but firmly, and Nelly, in the prime of womanhood, could as yet find nobody exactly to her taste. Mrs. Phipps, the aunt who had taken care of her since her mother's death, began to fear that she was destined for an old maid. Recalling her own youth, and its comparative scarcity of suitors, she wondered how her niece could be so impenetrable, and when, under the will of a cousin deceased, Miss Burton became possessed of a small independent fortune, the elder lady, arguing against her own interests and convenience, urged on the younger the propriety of at last settling in life.

Nelly did not seem to see it. When she could find leisure, and occasion offered, she was a reader of novels and a dreamer of dreams, though clear-headed and firm of purpose. She was also a thorough woman, and cherished deep in her heart those generous impulses of affection and romance which make much of a woman's pleasure in life, and all her pain. She had formed her ideal hero, who in no way resembled the men she was in the habit of meeting in her aunt's private sitting-room, or at the bar of the Corner Hotel, Corner Street, Strand. She had not settled exactly what he *was*, but had made up her mind what he was *not*.

In business? No. A mere idler? No. Young, slim, and genteel? No. Short, stout, and well - to - do? A thousand times no. Rather, a man of a certain age, a certain standing, who had seen the world, and thought things out, and been unhappy—perhaps about some other woman. She wouldn't mind that, a sore heart was better than none at all; and —and—she felt if she really loved him, she could console him for anything!

When we think of a woman's nature— excitable, imaginative, and in its affections

wholly unreasonable; when we think of a
girl's dreams—tender, unselfish, and thoroughly
unattainable—the wonder is, not that here and
there we shall find an unhappy marriage, but
that any two people, thoroughly disappointed
and undeceived, should be able to tolerate each
other kindly and comfortably to the end.
Even for men there is an awakening from the
rosy dream, usually within two years; but
they have so many interests and occupations
into which the affections do not enter, that
they prosper well enough without these super-
fluities, and prefer, I believe, the bracing air
and enforced activity of the working world, to
an oppressive atmosphere and irksome repose
in a fool's paradise. But it is far different
with their wives. Piece by piece the woman
sees her knight stripped of his golden armour;
feather by feather does her love-bird moult its
painted plumes, and the lower he falls in her
estimation, the higher this disappointing mate
seems to rise in his own. He kissed her feet
while she thought him a prince, he tramples

on her now she knows him a clown. After taming an eagle, it does seem humiliating to be coerced by an owl.

And there is no salvage; all her cargo has gone down in one ship. Is it wonderful that she looks abroad over the dreary waters, with a blank face and a troubled eye? Women are deceived over and over again. They like it; but even the pure gold never rings quite true in their ears when they have once been cheated by the counterfeit coin.

It seems an ungenerous sentiment, but I think that man is wise who does not allow his wife to know him thoroughly; who keeps back a reserve of strength, of authority, even of affection, for the hour of need, causing her to feel that there are depths in his character she has not yet sounded, heights she has not scaled. Thus can he indulge and keep alive her feline propensity to prowl, and pounce, and capture; thus will he remain an object of interest, of anxiety, of devotion; thus will she continue to see him through the coloured glass of her own imagination, and it will be the happier for both, because when affection goes to sleep in security, it is apt to forget all about waking, and those are the most enduring attachments in which the woman loves best of the two.

In the mean time Nelly has posted her letter, and paid the penny that entitled her to inhale sea-breezes on the pier.

It is an autumn day—delightful at the sea-side—with a bright sun, a crisp air, and a curl on the shining waters. All the visitors at Beachmouth seem to have turned out, though it is hardly eleven o'clock; but in the hundred or so of strangers who constitute this accidental population, there are none to be compared with Miss Burton.

Even the ladies stare at her as she walks on, and admit, frankly enough, that she "has a fine figure for people who admire that style. What a pity she must become coarse, even blowsy, in a year or two; and after all, it's very easy to be good-looking, with dark eyes, and all that quantity of hair, probably false ! "

The approval of the men, however, is unanimous. One youth, wearing a complete shooting-suit, that will never go out shooting, passes, re-passes, looks, leers, and seems about to speak; but Nelly is used to admiration, considering it, like beef or mutton, unpalatable unless properly cooked, and looking straight before her, gives him to understand by her bearing that she is the last person with whom he may presume to take a liberty.

Then she establishes herself at the extreme end of the jetty, as far out at sea as she can get, perhaps three hundred feet, and pulling some work from her pocket, gives herself up to the full enjoyment of air and scenery, with no more self-consciousness than the grey gull flapping and fishing not a cable's length from where she sits. Meanwhile, John Roy, deceived by a dress and a *chignon*, has walked two miles along the beach in pursuit of a figure that sets his heart beating while he

overtakes it, but on nearer inspection turns out
to be an elderly lady, ordered strong exercise
for her health, who meets his disappointed
stare with a perfectly unmeaning smile, and
a face shining in perspiration under the
noon-day sun.

CHAPTER IV.

DEEPER AND DEEPER.

EVENTS seldom come off exactly as people anticipate; yet the odds are longer than we think on the success of a man who expends all his energies in pursuit of any one object, great or small.

The old foxhunter's advice, "Keep your temper, and stick to the line," is a golden rule for the conduct of more serious affairs than bringing "the little red rover" to hand after all the delights and uncertainties of a run. If we carry on the metaphor into a love-chase, we shall find it even more appropriate to the gardens of Venus than the woodlands of Diana. Command of temper is everything in dealing with a woman's caprice, and that undeviating persistency which men call pigheadedness, and gods perseverance, seldom fails, sooner or later, to come up with and capture its prey. John Roy resolved to keep his temper, though he had overrun the line; and like a thorough woodsman, adapting his tactics to the habits of his game, he determined to " try back " without loss of time. But the pier was deserted when he arrived there, and he sat down to consider his next move, disappointed rather than disheartened. As he told himself, with something of sarcasm, " He was only hotter on it than before."

The tide would be out in the afternoon. He reflected that no woman, on her first day at the sea-side, could resist the temptation of wetting her feet in the little pools of salt water left, as if on purpose, by its ebb.

So after luncheon he watched, patiently enough, and having seen his friend of the morning packed into a watering-place fly, felt confident he would be deceived by that staunch pedestrian no more.

Presently he was rewarded. Not ten paces

from the rock where he had settled himself.
Forty-Six came stepping jauntily by, looking
steadfastly seaward while she drank in the
fresh briny air with a thirst engendered by
long months of London smoke and gas.

He could not but observe how true were
the lines of her undulating figure, how firmly
she planted her foot, how nobly she carried her
head, how smooth and level was her gait, as
she stepped bravely out across the sand.

"Watch, and your chance comes!" muttered
Roy, throwing away the cigar he was in the act
of lighting; for an occasion offered itself when
least expected, and he seized it without diffidence or hesitation. Two children enjoying, as
only children can, the delight of wooden spades
and low water, had wandered, I need hardly
say, to the extreme verge of safety, and far
beyond dry rocks, in pursuit of the receding
waves. Bare-footed and kilted high above
their fat little knees, they shouted, screamed,
and splashed to their hearts' content, while the
nurse, seated under an umbrella with her back

to them, was lost in the pages of a novel. They were boy and girl, the latter being the younger, and, if possible, the wilder of the two. In her frolics she found herself parted from her brother, and to her young perceptions cut off from society in general by a runlet of water nearly two feet deep. Becoming gradually alive to the horrors of her situation, she grasped her frock tight in both hands, and roared with all her might. The boy, who perhaps was turned four, made some slight offer at a rescue, but the intervening gulf seemed too much for him, and he also set up a hideous outcry, while the nurse read calmly on.

Nelly loved children. Glancing on each side to make sure she was unobserved, but neglecting in her hurry to look back, she pulled her boots and stockings off in a few seconds, caught up her garments as best she might, and was wading knee-deep to the rescue before John Roy could interfere.

How handsome she looked, hugging the frightened child in her arms, and soothing it with that beautiful instinct of maternity which pervades her whole sex from the first moment they are big enough to handle a doll.

With hurried apologies and some blushing on both sides—for Roy was already hard hit, and Nelly had certainly been caught in deshabille—he took possession of the little girl, now completely reassured, and carried her safe to the nurse, studiously turning his back on Miss Burton while she resumed her stockings. " He is a gentleman," thought Nelly, " every inch of him. I dare say he's a good fellow, too, he seems so fond of children."

Such an introduction was equivalent to a week's acquaintance. With a little shyness, a little hesitation and incoherence of speech, the gentleman and lady managed to communicate their respective names, and to digest the startling intelligence that they were staying at the same hotel, that it was comfortable but might be cleaner, that the sea-air made one hungry, and the roar of the tide kept one awake—all which facts were self-evident, and in no way accounted for the low tones, grave accents, or downcast glances with which they were propounded and received.

It seemed imprudent, too, for people with wet feet, to walk home at an exceedingly slow pace, and halt so repeatedly on the way.

Each thought the distance had been much longer, and both said so at the same moment. Then came more bowing, more blushing, an abortive attempt at shaking hands, and an imbecile, unmeaning kind of parting, that left John Roy standing in the entrance-hall with his mouth open and his heart in it, while Nelly hurried upstairs to take refuge in 46.

Her first impulse, though by no means a vain person, was to look in the glass. What she saw there caused her to smile, sigh, and shake her head. Then she sat down on the bed to think.

Mr. Roy, on the other hand, turned into the coffee-room, and ordered dinner for seven o'clock, with an indifference to the bill of fare that disgusted and a positiveness that surprised the waiter—securing also a table near the clock, at one end of the room.

For the next two or three days, everything "went upon wheels." If people are inclined to like each other and live in the same hotel at a small watering-place it is probable they will meet many times in the twenty-four hours. Twice, at least, between breakfast and dinner on the Pier, without counting accidental encounters on the stairs, in the streets, under the portico of the Circulating Library, by the ebb and flow of the soothing tide, or at sunset on the beach. It is surprising how soon an idea, canvassed, cherished, and combated by turns, takes entire possession of the mind. The first day of their acquaintance Mr. Roy and Miss Burton felt that a new element of interest had entered into life. The second, they were perfectly happy; quiet, contented, asking nothing better than to remain undisturbed. The third, both had grown restless, fidgetty, dissatisfied, and a crisis was near.

It had become an established custom that

they should meet in their walks, they had even started together from the hotel. On one occasion, however, Miss Burton went out by herself, and took up a position at the extreme end of the Pier. As she stated openly, that this was her favourite resort, it is not surprising Mr. Roy should have followed with no more delay than was required to run upstairs and get his hat.

The band had ceased playing, children and nurses were gone home to dinner, these two had the Pier to themselves. Perhaps that was why they became so silent, so pre-occupied, believing they were perfectly happy, yet feeling somewhat ill-at-ease.

After the first meeting, a hypocritical " good-morning," that had already been exchanged in the hotel corridor, neither spoke for two or three minutes, which seemed like two or three hours. Nelly had forgotten her work, Roy did not even attempt to smoke, and they sat side by side staring at a grey gull who stuck diligently to his fishing, without noticing a feather of his wings.

"Miss Burton, shouldn't you like to be a gull?" asked Roy presently, with a much more serious face than the question seemed to require.

"Mr. Roy, shouldn't you like to be a goose?" was the reply that naturally presented itself; but Nelly only answered in rather a shaking voice, "Yes, I should, because it can stay at the sea-side as long as it likes."

"And can't *you?*" said Roy, taking the alarm.

She shook her head.

"I don't live here, you know. I only came down for a visit; and I have dawdled on, expecting my aunt to fetch me home. I am afraid now she will be prevented. And— and, I think I ought to go back to London at once,"—the last in a low tone, looking steadfastly out to sea.

"Don't you like Beachmouth?"

"Oh, yes; very much."

" Haven't you been happy since you came here ? "

" Yes ; very happy. I am so fond of the sea-air, and the bathing, and the walks on the sands. I have enjoyed it extremely ; I shall be quite sorry to go away."

" Only for that ? "

Her head was averted. She felt her heart beating fast, and the colour rising ˙scarlet to her face.

" Miss Burton."

No answer.

" Miss Burton," he repeated, clearing his voice with a husky little cough, " I hope, I say, I *hope* there is something here you will be sorry to leave, besides the bathing and the sands. I cannot expect you to feel about it as I do ; but—but—whether you go or stay, I must tell you the truth. Ever since the first night I saw you at dinner, I—I have thought you the handsomest, and the dearest, and the nicest woman in the world."

" Lor ! "

Was it a disillusion? He hardly knew.
Lady Jane, he remembered, under similar
circumstances, exclaimed, "How *can* you be so
foolish?" But at any rate he had got the
steam on, and it was too late to stop now.

"I have not much to offer," he continued.
"I am many years older than you. I am
asking a great deal, with little to give in
return. You will say we hardly know each
other; but I should not be the least afraid for
the future, if you thought you could learn to
like me after a while. Perhaps I ought to
have waited longer before speaking, but when
you said you were going away it put me off
my guard. I could not bear to lose my second
chance in life. It is only right to tell you. I
know what disappointment is; I loved another
woman once."

"Only once?"

He knew he was winning now, and stole
his hand into hers. "Only once," he repeated,
"and it was many years ago. If you would
be my wife, I would try to make you happy.

Do you think, *don't* you think, Miss Burton, if I tried very hard I might succeed?"

"Don't call me Miss Burton. People I like call me Nelly."

"And you like *me*?"

"Yes, I do."

"And you will learn to love me in time?" His arm was round her waist now, and her head rested on his shoulder.

"I've learned it already. I've loved you ever so long. Ever since the day before yesterday. Let go of me, please, there's somebody coming on the Pier!"

CHAPTER V.

For the last few days Miss Burton had sadly neglected her only correspondent. It was so difficult to write without alluding to the subject that filled her heart, and she had never kept anything from Aunt Matilda in her life. Now she could tell triumphantly and without reserve what a lucky woman she was, and how happy. Dear Auntie would be so pleased and so proud when she learned that her niece was going to be a real lady. I am afraid Nelly called it "a lady of position." How Auntie would admire Mr. Roy! his well-cut clothes, his upright figure, his white hands, and his gallant bearing. She would declare he looked like a lord; and so he did, as there was no earthly reason why he should not. It seemed impossible to realise the fact that she, Nelly Burton, was going to belong to this paragon, this phœnix, this king of men! How she loved him, how she doted on him, now that it was no longer humiliating nor unwomanly to admit her affection! Every line of his worn face, every turn of his manly figure, every tone of his quiet, decided voice, suggested the breeding, the education, and the unconscious self-respect of a gentleman. Yes, to the bookseller's daughter, in this consisted his irresistible attraction. He was the embodiment of her ideal, and that ideal had always presented itself as identified with a higher social class than her own. He was the realisations of her dreams, and if she might belong to him, nay, as she *must* belong to him, how could she worship him enough? What an exquisite and subtle flattery was conveyed in this confession that she had fascinated him at once; that he, who might take his choice, as she implicitly believed, of all the ladies at her Majesty's drawing-room, should have fallen in love with

her, so he declared, from the moment he saw
the back of her head.   This was surely love
at first sight, of which she had read, and
heard, and pondered, but never hoped to
experience the charm.   It seemed as if nobody
had a right to be so happy, and she walked up
and down the room in a transport that was
only modified by those vague misgivings, that
shadowy sense of uncertainty, with which,
from the very constitution of our nature, must
be tempered all extremes of earthly joy.   Then
she fell on her knees to thank God, with wet
eyes, for her exceeding happiness, and so, in a
more composed frame of mind, took out her
blotting-book and wrote a letter to her Aunt.

        " DEAREST AUNTIE,

            " I have such a piece of news !   You
will never guess, not if you try for a month.
You must have wondered why I wrote so
seldom, and thought me the most ungrateful
minx in the world.   No; you would never
think that.   But you may have fancied I was

ill. If so, forgive me for having caused you a moment's anxiety. Dear Auntie, I feel as if I should never be ill again. I am so happy; *so* happy! Do you remember the American gentleman who declared the whole of out-of-doors wasn't big enough to contain his disgust? Well, I feel exactly the same about my happiness. I certainly am the luckiest girl, or rather the luckiest woman, in the universe!

" You have often told me I ought to marry, and I always said, No. It used to seem such an easy word. But I couldn't have got it out to-day if my life depended on it, and that little syllable once spoken would have made two people miserable for ever. Any how, I can answer for *one!* But I am keeping you on tenter-hooks, when I ought to make my confession. Dearest Auntie, I am going to be married! There! Now the cat is out of the bag! And to the noblest, the dearest, the kindest, the handsomest of men. To explain it all I must begin at the beginning.

" The night I came here, it seems such a

long time ago now, and it isn't really more
than a week, I asked to have some tea upstairs,
but I saw they didn't want to send it, so I
ordered dinner in the coffee-room, smoothed
my hair, and went down, not best pleased to
think I should find myself alone amongst a lot
of strangers. Would you believe it, only three
other tables were laid, and I sat with my back
to them all, so I had my dinner comfortable
without noticing anybody. There was one
gentleman I couldn't help seeing, when I got
up to go away, and I won't deny that I
thought him a fine, straight-made fellow, with
white hands, dark eyes, and hair just turning
grey, but I didn't notice him much, as you
may suppose. However, I *do* believe there is
a fate in these things. The very next day I
had an adventure, and Mr. Roy—that's his
name, Auntie, you'll know it better soon—.
appeared as the hero. I was down on the
sands, you may be sure, and I happened to see
a child hemmed in by streams of salt water
that would have reached to its poor little neck.

Such a darling, Auntie, with great blue eyes
and beautiful fair hair! Well, I don't like to
think of it even now, but I whipped my boots
and stockings off, and waded in at once to this
poor little Robinson Crusoe, thinking nobody
was looking, or perhaps not thinking at all, for
the child seemed so frightened there was no
time to lose. I soon had it in my arms, hiding
its dear little face on my shoulder, and there
was Mr. Roy, splashing through the water,
clothes and all, to take it from me and carry it
to the nurse. I thought I should have
dropped, only one never *does* drop, I felt so
put out and ashamed that a gentleman should
have caught me without shoes and stockings,
like a barefooted gipsy swinging on a gate.
Dear fellow! He has confessed since he
watched me all the way from the hotel. I
didn't know it then. I suppose I should have
been very angry, but I am not angry the least.
I shall never be angry with *him* all my life now.

"We walked home together, and though
he was very kind and polite, hoping I would

not take cold with my wetting, he didn't say much. I never supposed that he thought of me for a moment, at least in *that* way, till to-day.

"I'm not going to deny that I admired him, and was foolish enough to wish sometimes there could be a chance of our meeting after I left Beachmouth; but I kept my wishes to myself, and didn't even tell *you*, dear Auntie, what a silly I could be when I am old enough to know better. And yet, as things have turned out, I wasn't such a great silly after all.

"You have been married yourself, Auntie, and had lots of followers, I dare say, before you changed your name, so you know how it all comes about. At first it only seemed strange and rather pleasant to meet Mr. Roy by accident wherever I went; then I began to think he did it on purpose, and I felt I ought not to encourage him. One day I walked right away into the country, but I couldn't resist turning back at the first milestone when I thought of his disappointed face hunting for me all over the beach and the Pier. Then I knew I was beginning to care for him, and I determined to go away from here at once.

"That was only yesterday; to-day everything is different. I went to the window after breakfast, and watched him out of the house, as I said to myself, for the *last* time, meaning directly his back was turned to take my own walk in an opposite direction.

"I cried a little; I'm not ashamed to confess it now. Wasn't it stupid? And I shall be thirty next birthday. When he was fairly started I bathed my eyes, put on my hat, and trudged off to the Pier. There was no harm in taking a last look at everything, but I felt very *down*, though I had quite made up my mind to go.

"I wonder how he knew! I hadn't been there ten minutes before I heard his step. I didn't need to turn my head; I can tell his walk among a thousand; and it seemed so natural for him to sit down by me and look at the sea, that I could have burst out crying again when I thought it was all for the *last* time.

"I don't know how he came to say it, Auntie, but he *did* say it. I don't know exactly what he said, and if I could repeat it I shouldn't, even to *you;* but he confessed he cared very much for me, and asked me to be his wife. That's enough, and more than enough, for me!

"Nothing is settled. Most likely it's too great happiness and will never be—that won't influence *my* feelings. I promised him faithful, and if I am not to belong to him, I'll belong to nobody, and die an old maid.

"So now I have told you all about it. There is little more to be said. I think I ought to leave this at once. It will be too late to get an answer, or I would ask your advice, though a woman don't want anybody to advise her in such a matter as this. I shall be off by the early train to-morrow morning; you will not be taken by surprise, as this ought to reach you first post. If Mr. Roy means fair, he will soon follow. When I say 'if,' don't suppose I have any doubts. Could I believe he was false, I think I should just pay my penny once more, walk to the end of the Pier, and never come back again!

"What a long letter! Wish me joy when I see you to-morrow, and believe me

"Always your loving niece,

"ELINOR BURTON."

No date, of course, but crossed, re-crossed, and filled to the edges. When Miss Burton had slipped it into the hotel letter-box she returned to her room, and spent the rest of the evening packing up her clothes.

John Roy, wandering to and fro like a disturbed spirit, felt grievously hurt and discomposed that after an interview which had such decided results, he should see no more of his promised wife during the rest of the day. Though a man cultivates less subtle feelings of delicacy than a woman, his better nature told him she was right. Nevertheless, like the rest of us when we are dissatisfied with our gourd, he followed the example of Jonah, and thought he "did well to be angry."

His wrath however was mollified, and the re-action made him more in love than ever, when going to his room before dinner he found a pretty little note pinned on his toilet-cover, the address of which was written in the clearest and most beautiful characters ever beheld. He kissed it once *before* reading it, I should be afraid to say how often, after.

" My dear Sir, or

" My dear Mr. Roy, or

" My dear Friend,—What am I to call you? Do not be surprised that I write a few lines, instead of seeing you before I go, to say good-bye. I cannot explain why, but I feel that after what took place to-day, I ought to return home at once. I hope you will not be hurt, and I am sure you will not be offended. I think, on reflection, it is what you would like me to do yourself. I shall not go down to dinner, and I shall leave to-morrow morning for my aunt's house, Corner Hotel, Corner Street, Strand. I wonder whether you will remember the address. Even if you do not, even if I am never to see you again, believe me always so long as I live,

". Your own

" NELLY."

" P.S. It is rather an early start. I must be at the station by 7.30."

She *was* at the station by 7.30, and so was Mr. Roy. Having ascertained, we need not inquire how, that Miss Burton drank tea with the landlady the previous evening, who afterwards assisted in finishing her packing and saw her safe to bed, he had the good taste to anticipate her at the station instead of accompanying her from the hotel, and made his farewell on the platform, where indeed at that early hour there were but few lookers-on.

"And when shall I see you again?" said

he, after a warm though hurried renewal of certain protestations that he felt had been unjustly curtailed.

"It depends on yourself," was the reply, while she gave him both hands with a look of confidence and affection that made her handsomer than ever. "I shall wait for you at my aunt's—waiting—always waiting—if you never come, I shall wait for you just the same."

"I *hate* waiting," said he. "If I had my own way, you shouldn't wait a minute. Why can't I get my ticket and go with you now?"

She smiled and shook her head. "Why?" she repeated. "I'm sure I don't know *why*. And yet I feel it would put me in a false position; you see it would not be right."

"I *don't* see. Why wouldn't it?"

"Because it wouldn't!" And though this was a woman's reason, it seemed to him convincing and unanswerable, as based on some instinct of truth deeper and more infallible than all the inductions of philosophy, and all the wisdom of the schools.

CHAPTER VI.

SO LIKE A MAN!

STORM and calm, rain and sunshine, bitter and sweet, action and reaction, are not these the conditions of life? If the wind is fair to-day, look for it in your teeth to-morrow; what is earned by the right hand, you are bound to spend with the left, and never expect to be four-by-honours in two deals running!

Who so happy as an accepted lover? He treads on air, he mounts to the skies, and he soars on the wings of a dove, believing firmly that he has abjured the wisdom of the serpent for evermore. Yet after the first access of transport, every succeeding moment brings him down, nearer and nearer the ground, till at last he walks about again on two legs, like a husband, or a goose, or any other biped, having neither energy nor inclination to fly.

I need not say that John Roy bade adieu to Beachmouth, betook himself to Charing Cross Station, and proceeded thence to the Corner Hotel, Corner Street, Strand, without loss of time. The · distance was short. He could almost have wished it longer, that he might gain more time to realise the step he had taken.

Like most English gentlemen, he was a bold fellow enough on a horse, in a row, under any circumstances of risk to life or limb, but he was also sensitive and shy, particularly with inferiors, shrinking from their approaches, as a timid woman shrinks from observation and personal address.

It was not reassuring to find the hotel door blocked up by an arrival, or to be told . without hesitation, by a supercilious waiter in yesterday's white neckcloth, that they were full to the garrets, and hadn't a bed · unoccupied, while he volunteered with something of reproof the further information that this was a private hotel, and if the gentleman expected to find accommodation he should have written to Mrs. Phipps at least a week ago.

" But I don't want a room," said John Roy, out of patience; " I came here to call on Miss—, I mean, is Mrs. Phipps at home? "

" Mrs. Phipps is engaged."

" Go and tell her that a gentleman wishes to see her particularly, and will not detain her five minutes."

John Roy was peremptory, not to say stern ; but the waiter stood to his guns.

" Any name, sir? " as if a man without a portmanteau must also be without a name.

The visitor wished he had brought a card-case.

" Mr. Roy," said he, " and be so good as to go at once. I don't choose to be kept waiting half-an-hour on the door-step."

But Nelly, who was already in the passage, flew to the threshold, and welcomed him with

such warmth and cordiality as completely re
assured the waiter.

"I *knew* you would come!" she whispered.
"I have been expecting you all the morning.
This way. Mind the step. Don't run against
the coal-box. We're so full, we have been
driven down-stairs. We generally live in the
front dining-room. Now, I'll bring you in,
and show you to Auntie."

The charm was working again, and at high
pressure. So lovely, so loving, so bright, so
beautiful, above all, so glad to see him. Who
would not have followed such a guide down
the darkest passages, the most inconvenient
stairs that ever smelt of mould, soap, sawdust,
stale coffee, and early dinner?

Mrs. Phipps was an excellent woman, no
doubt—clear-headed, bustling, full of energy,
a capital accountant, sincere, sensible, with a
heart of gold—but she was *not* exactly the sort
of person John Roy would have selected for
his wife's aunt.

He had a keen sense of the ludicrous, and

as she came forward, rubbing one hand over
the other, to stop in front of him, with a
profound curtsey, he took in her exterior at a
glance. The dark dress, looking dingier in the
obscurity of a room on the basement, lighted
from a grating in the pavement outside. The
portliness of figure, increasing as it travelled
upward to the chin; the large brooch, the
bright gold chain, the jet ornaments twinkling
in a solemn head-gear, black, pompous, and
funereal as the artificial tresses it surmounted,
and the plain oblong face, with just so much
resemblance to Nelly as might create a vague
and morbid fear lest her bright young beauty
should ever turn to this!

He made the best of it, and put out
both hands. "You are to be *my* aunt, too,"
said he. "Miss Burton has told you everything of course. I am always going to
call her Nelly for the future, and you must
learn to look upon me as a relation of your
own."

He was not prepared for the result. Mrs.

Phipps burst out crying, and put her arms round his neck.

After this little ebullition she became practical enough. "I'm sure it's a great honour," said she, "and a great happiness to . us all. It's what I never expected, and yet Nelly *do* deserve the best that ever wore shoe-leather, and I always said so. She was a good daughter, Mr. Roy, was Nelly, and a good niece. I'm sure I've reason to know it, and she'll make a good wife to the man who will be kind to her. I can see in your face as you're one of that sort. I'm a plain-spoken woman, Mr. Roy; I never had the manners of my niece there, nor yet the education. I've my bread to get, as I may say, by hard and honest work; but you won't think the worse of us, I hope; and you won't take it as a liberty if I say, 'God bless you both!' and I should like to shake you by the hand, Mr. Roy, once more."

So this ceremony was repeated, and Roy acknowledged to himself that the good old

woman who had educated his betrothed wife
was a thorough lady at heart, although she
spoke second-class English and kept an hotel.

"You'll take a glass of wine, Mr. Roy,"
continued his hostess, relapsing into her com-
mon-place mood. "I wish I could ask you to
stop dinner, but Nelly and me has had our
dinner, and you couldn't hardly see to eat it
neither in so dark a place as this. I wish I
wasn't so put about for room. But what am I
to do? You can't turn people away from the
doors, if you keep an hotel."

"Mr. Roy never takes wine in the day-
time, Auntie," said Nelly, assuming entire
charge of his habits, as became a woman
engaged for more than twenty-four hours.
"We can give him a cup of tea in five
minutes, and I'll make it myself; I know what
he likes better than you do."

But Mr. Roy preferred a walk with Nelly
to refreshment of any kind, and the pair were
soon strolling arm-in-arm along that romantic
thoroughfare, the Strand, discussing *trousseaux*,

wedding, honeymoon, their eventual future.
What do I know? What do people talk about
when they are going to be married and lead a
new life?

So the weeks went on. John Roy found
himself waking morning after morning with a
strange, anxious feeling that he was yet a day
nearer his fate, sometimes impatient to get it
over, sometimes thinking he could wait as long
as he pleased, but never wavering in his
loyalty to Nelly, nor allowing, for one second,
that he regretted his choice.

It was the dead time of year. " Not a soul
in London," said the souls who met the other
souls in the street, yet is the Great City seldom
so empty, even of rich and idle, but that ten
or twelve can be got together for a dinner-
party at short notice. There *are* people who
profess they like these little gatherings better
than the crowd and hurry of the season, declaring that they never enjoy the society of
their friends so thoroughly as when " there is
nobody in town ! "

In St. James Street and Pall Mall might
be found a few lingerers, dull and torpid as the
winter flies on a window-pane, but the Park
seemed unusually deserted. Perhaps for that
reason it was the chosen resort of Mr. Roy and
Miss Burton, who would turn in at Albert
Gate, having arrived there, as became a regularly engaged couple, in a hansom cab, to walk
in the Ride, or sit down and make plans for
the future, while she looked in his face with
adoring eyes, and he—well—he smoked, and
let her look.

"I *like* this," whispered Nelly, pressing
closer to his side as they returned one day
from an hour or two of the above engrossing
occupation. "You and me have got it all to
ourselves!"

"It," meant that stretch of rugged bricks
and rubbish, with a surface of mud just thick
enough to splash, which the Government then
in office had provided for its tax-payers on
horseback, and seemed in so far a solitude
when Nelly spoke that its only other occupants

were a fat man on a cob, and a doubtful-looking lady riding a lame horse.

"It's very nice," answered John Roy, rather preoccupied, for just then a figure turned into the Ride on a hunting-looking chestnut, at a pace that promised soon to bring him alongside our pedestrians. The easy seat and general outline were not to be mistaken. Roy wished at the moment he had some other lady on his arm.

The chestnut though going fast must have been well in hand, it was pulled up so quickly at the rails, while a familiar voice exclaimed, "Hulloh, Roy! In town at this time of year! Come and dine to-day. I'm off to-morrow morning for Newmarket." Then, as if catching sight of Nelly for the first time, the speaker bowed to his stirrup-iron, and added, "I *beg* your pardon. I was so glad to see my friend!"

It stung Roy to feel there should be an absolute necessity for introducing her on the spot as "Miss Burton—a lady who is going to do me the honour of becoming my wife." It

stung him still more to notice an instantaneous
change of manner, that only a sensitive nature
would have detected, while with a second bow,
not quite so low, yet somehow more respectful,
the other observed, "Then it's no use hoping
for you at dinner. Allow me to congratulate
you both!" and cantered off.

"What a pretty fellow!" said Nelly, in a
tone of undisguised admiration.

"Most women agree with you," answered
Roy, wondering he was not more nettled.
"They used to call him the lady-killer in his
regiment."

Her grey eyes opened wide.

"Did he really kill a lady? How horrible!
He ought never to be saddled again!"

John Roy laughed. "You mean the horse,
dear," said he. "I thought it was the man."

"Oh! I never looked at the gentleman,"
answered Nelly. "Who is he? What's his
name?"

"Lord Fitzowen—commonly called Fitz!"

"A lord, is he? Well, he don't look half

so like a lord as you! What is he going to Newmarket for?"

John Roy did not answer. He was thinking it would be rather up-hill work to teach his wife all the ins-and-outs, the little technicalities, the very language of that artificial world into which he was bringing her. They would live in the country, he determined, and come but little to London for the present. A man might be very happy in the country with some hunting, shooting, farming, and such a beautiful creature to keep his house. One couldn't have everything. It was a great piece of good fortune that he didn't marry Lady Jane!

And Nelly, clinging to his arm, wondered how she could ever have lived without him. His presence was paradise, his absence a blank. All places were alike if she only had *him* by her side.

So they were married in due course of time —exactly one month from the day that he proposed to her on Beachmouth Pier. The wedding was quiet enough. No bishop, no bridesmaids, and a cake of small dimensions from the confectioner's round the corner. The happy couple walked quietly out of the hotel to a neighbouring church. Nelly was given away by her nearest male relation, a retired drysalter residing at Clapham, who felt and looked in a false position throughout. Mrs. Phipps wept plentifully in the rector's pew (absent with his family in Switzerland), and the ceremony was performed by an ecclesiastic, somewhat irreverently mentioned as " a clergyman on a job." One very old shoe was thrown by the upper housemaid when the happy couple left the hotel in a cab, and the waiter remained drunk all day. These were the only festivities. The servants agreed that though Miss Burton had done well for herself, the bridegroom looked old enough to be her father, and the wedding was a tame affair!

Nevertheless, it was over, and they were married as irrevocably and completely as if a primate had officiated, and the whole House of Lords had signed the register.

Nelly was supremely happy; so, in a calmer degree, was her husband. Both had obtained that to which most people look forward as the crowning joy of life, yet it seemed like a dream to read in next day's *Times* the simple and unpretending notice—

"Yesterday, at St. Withold's, by the Rev. Joseph Makeshift—JOHN ROY, Esq., of Royston Grange and 907, Piccadilly, to ELINOR, sole surviving daughter of Jacob Burton, Esq., late of High Holborn, London."

"John Roy?" said one or two friends, gleaning the morning papers with cigars in their mouths—"I have often wondered what had become of him. Used to be rather a good fellow. Only surviving child, too; looks as if he had picked up an heiress. Great absurdity marrying after forty, and infernal mistake to get caught before!"

But Nelly's history only began in reality on the day when she felt she was the happiest woman in the world because she stood at the altar as Roy's wife.

CHAPTER VII.

"AND you know her, Lord Fitzowen? What an odd person you are! I believe you know everybody in the world."

"I thought you said she was *out* of the world, Miss Bruce. Therefore you were surprised I should have made her acquaintance."

"That's not the question. Where *can* you have met her?"

"Nothing more simple; walking in the Park with her husband."

"Before they were married?"

"Of course. People don't walk together in the Park after they're married, unless they've had a row."

"And he introduced you?"

"Why shouldn't he? Won't you introduce

me to *your* husband, Miss Bruce, when the
time comes and the man ? "

.   She smiled, rather wistfully, " Perhaps you
know him already," said she. " And if you
don't, I am not sure you are a desirable
acquaintance. You might lead him into
mischief."

" Somebody has been maligning me, and
to *you* of all people, in whose good opinion I
want so much to stand high. An enemy has
done this."

" Not Mrs. Roy, at any rate. She couldn't
remember having seen you. I said you were
here, and asked her. There, Lord Fitz ! There's
a come-down ! "

" Not a bit. Say a see-saw, if you please ;
for it's a go-up at the other end. If *she* had
forgotten me, *you* hadn't ! "

" How *can* I forget you when you're staying
in the house? Besides, don't flatter yourself
that I ever try ! "

" Then I'll wait for a more favourable
opportunity, and we'll talk about something

else. What did you think of your new neighbour?"

"What did *you*?"

"I thought her—charming!"

"How like a man! As if that conveyed
anything. Now I will do you justice, Lord
Fitz. I believe you pretend to be stupider
than you are, so I wonder you didn't find
out something."

"What was there to find out? I could
see with my own eyes she hadn't a wooden
leg."

"Indeed! Well, you'll say I am ill-natured,
and that one woman always tries to disparage
another; did it not strike you she is hardly
quite a lady? I don't mean to say she drops
her h's, but something very like it. She has
never lived amongst the people you and I are
accustomed to meet, and I think Mr. Roy
feels it. He looked very black at her more
than once."

"What a shame! They haven't been married
six weeks. If I had a wife now—never mind

—I'm not going to commit myself, Miss Bruce.
I might say too much."

" If you *had* a wife of course you would be
just as trying as other husbands, but that's no
business of mine.   I was going to tell you—
when we called, papa and I, as we were bound
to do at once, being such near neighbours, we
found them at home, and I know she was got-
up to receive visitors.   In fact, she told me so.
She called it "seeing company."   She was well
dressed, I must say, not *too* well, and as handsome as a picture.   You seldom see such eyes
and hair.   But for all that, there's a something.
I'm convinced she is not what I call *thorough-
bred*, and yet papa wouldn't allow it.   He was
completely fascinated, and you know how
particular he is."

" Naturally.   If I were *your* papa, I should
be very particular indeed."

" Nonsense.   Don't interrupt.   I watched
Mr. Roy, and I'm sure he wasn't at his ease.
He looked in a fidget every time she opened
her mouth.   I was sorry for him, and we

didn't stay long, though she pressed me to *take* luncheon, and to *take* tea, and hoped I wouldn't *take* cold in the open carriage, and all the rest of it, as kindly as possible."

"And have you taken cold—I beg your pardon—*caught* cold? for if so, you had better not stand here any longer. I shouldn't like your death to lie at my door."

"You haven't got a door, only a latch-key. But for once you talk sense. So draw my skates a little tighter, and we'll practise the Dutchman's Roll round the island and back again. Are you ready? Go!"

During the performance of this exhibition, which is but a succession of outside edges, neither very speedy nor very graceful, I may take the opportunity of explaining how these young people came to be disporting themselves on some five acres of ice, which milder weather would dissolve into a pretty little lake, forming a principal ornament in the grounds of Warden Towers.

Sir Hector and Miss Bruce, a widower and

an only daughter, had come to reside here, as their neighbours hoped, for a permanence, having taken a long lease of the place, which, notwithstanding its somewhat feudal name, had been hitherto the home of a retired tradesman, whose asthma compelled him to fight for breath in a warmer climate elsewhere. The house, though built with a turret at each end, was handsome and comfortable, the park roomy enough for a gallop, but not so extensive as to admit of feeding deer, and the gardens were exceedingly well laid out. As Sir Hector observed, " It was a nice gentlemanlike place in which to drivel away the rest of one's life. If Hester liked it, he would never ask to sleep out of the chintz room in the east tower again."

Hester liked whatever suited papa—that is to say, she turned him round her white fingers as an only daughter does turn the father who has learned to believe her a prodigy of infancy, a paragon of girlhood, and in all respects a pearl·among womankind. Sir Hector, though his Christian and surnames sounded so warlike, was a mild old gentleman of rather convivial habits and an easy temper, even when tortured by gout. He accepted its pains and penalties with a good humour that roused the admiration of his friends; and the moment he resumed the use of his hands, or could put his lame feet to the ground, returned to those indulgences that sustained and strengthened his enemy with a zest only sharper for remembrance of past discipline and prospect of future pain.

To be sure, as he used to declare, "It was a pleasure to be ill when one could have Hester for a nurse;" and it is but justice to say that no temptation could lure this young lady from her post if papa was either threatened or laid up. Many a time she stripped off riding-habit or ball-dress and sent the carriage back from the very door at the first of those symptoms that her experience told her were forerunners of an attack. Many an hour did she pass in darkened rooms, measuring draughts, smoothing pillows, reading to him, talking to

him, soothing the sufferer with her presence
and the touch of her hand, when other girls
were sunning themselves in the looks of their
admirers at archery-meeting and picnic, or,
more delightful still, enjoying a stirring gallop
under soft November skies, over lush November
pastures, after the hounds!

For in such amusements and pastimes did
Miss Bruce take more than a masculine delight.
Lithe, straight, and agile, she was a proficient
in all those bodily exercises at which ladies
are now able to compete on equal terms with
the stronger sex. A practised whip, she drove
her ponies to an inch; a capital horsewoman,
she rode to hounds (with a good pilot) in the
first flight. She danced like a fairy; could
run a quarter of a mile or walk half-a-dozen,
without the slightest inconvenience, and even
professed, though of this she afforded no actual
proof, that she was able to jump a gate or a
stile. At any rate, for all her softness of manner and grace of bearing, she seemed tough as
whalebone, and nimble as a wild deer.

In these days of high-pressure education she could not but be full of accomplishments, playing scientific music at sight, singing a second, speaking three or four languages, idiomatically, ungrammatically, and with a fair accent. She knew how to work embroidery, knit shooting-hose, and send people in to dinner according to their rank without fear of a mistake. On the other hand, she was but a moderate historian, sacred or profane, believed our version of the Bible a direct translation from the Hebrew, remembered the Wars of the Roses only because of their pretty name, and suffered hopeless confusion about the Ligue and the Fronde. She could *not* read Shakspeare, she honestly confessed, nor understand Tennyson, had tried to wade through "Corinne" and found it *stupid*, believed she would have liked Sir Walter but for the Scotch dialect, and thought in her heart "Vanity Fair" and the "Loves of the Angels" the two finest works in the language. Of household affairs she had some vague glimmerings, the result of

experience in ordering dinner, and even believed, because she never tried, that she could
do her own marketing.   Every Christmas she
spent a cheque from papa in soup and blankets,
which she gave away with a great deal of
method and very little judgment.   To sum up
all, she was a staunch Protestant, a regular
church-goer, and skated to admiration.

Her cavalier, also, performed handsomely
over ice or asphalte, on skates or rollers.   Both
were members of Prince's Club, nor does it
necessarily follow, as nameless slanderers would
have us believe, that they were therefore utterly
lost to all considerations of honourable feeling
and even outward decency.   It is difficult to
understand why a pastime that brings young
people together in a glare of light under the
eyes of countless spectators, should have been
held up to obloquy as a recognised means of
the vilest intrigue; or why a healthy exercise,
exacting close attention under considerable
effort, should be supposed to cloak overtures
and advances that might be made far less

conspicuously in the crash of a concert or the confusion of a ball-room.

It seems to me that the black sheep of both sexes must be at a disadvantage when the slightest inclination to either side from a just and equal balance cannot but result in physical downfall. The admirer deposited on his seat rather than his knees may scarcely hope to excite sympathy in his idol, and the idol herself must be well aware that she can never mount her pedestal again if she comes down from it with a sprawl! That Miss Bruce was as wicked a young lady as she was a good skater, I emphatically deny. For her companion's virtues I will not take upon me to answer with the same certainty.

Lord Fitzowen, as Mr. Roy said, "commonly called Fitz," had been about the world for more years than people thought, or, indeed, than he wished them to think.

He was one of those men, happily not very numerous in his order, who, after the first blush of youth, seem to have no object in the

world but to amuse themselves. For this
levity of disposition and indifference to the
real purposes of life he was perhaps indebted
to the joyous temperament that accompanies
perfect bodily health. A famous writer of our
own day has expressed the startling opinion
that if people never found their livers out of
order, no great works would be accomplished.
This is, perhaps, another way of saying that
discontent is the origin of progress.

As Fitz, from the time he pounded straw-
berry messes at Eton till he mixed Hussar-
broth (a compound of which the *substratum*
used to be red-herrings fried in gin) for his
brother subalterns at Hounslow, never knew he
had a liver, and hated, besides, every kind of
mental exertion, we may presume that nature
did not intend him for one of those "weary
brothers" who either imprint, or appreciate,
"footprints on the sands of time." What he
did—rather what he did *not* do, if we may be
allowed such a contradiction in terms—seemed
done remarkably well. He was the best idler

in society, and this is saying a good deal in London life where the art is cultivated with a diligence that cannot but ensure success.

Having a title, though an Irish one, a sufficient income, an agreeable person, imperturbable good-humour, and spirits, as he said himself, "forty above proof," it is no wonder that Lord Fitzowen was welcome everywhere, and an especial favourite amongst women.

Nevertheless, with an intuitive perception of the fitness of things, denied to the duller sex, they never expected him to marry. "He's delightful, I know, dear," Miss Bruce observed on one occasion in the confidence of five o'clock tea, "but as for anything serious, I should as soon expect a proposal from the beadle at St. George's. It's entirely out of Fitz's line!" So he made love to them all round without burning his fingers, and persuaded himself that, with many faults, he was yet a man of strong feelings and sincere affections.

Somehow Fitz always seemed to belong to the prettiest woman present. Although there

were other guests at Warden Towers, it was
characteristic that he alone should be gazing
at a winter sunset with his host's handsome
daughter after completing the Dutchman's Roll
to the unbounded satisfaction of both.

" It is time to go in," said Hester, rosy and
breathless, looking intently at the red streaks
fading into a frosty film behind the island.
" How I love this cold, clear weather !   I wish
it would last all the year through."

" You ought to have been an Arctic ex-
plorer," laughed Fitz.

Miss Bruce made no answer, but her eye
deepened and the smile faded from her face.

CHAPTER VIII.

ROYSTON GRANGE.

THE cold, clear weather soon began to change. The sun went down red and frosty, but Fitz, looking out of his bed-room window at midnight, observed a halo round the moon, which he described as "her wig," and by breakfast-time a thaw was proclaimed. Spouts trickled, eaves dripped, birds chirped in the laurels, the distant downs melted into grey, and a soft wind blew gently through the fir plantations on the south of Warden Towers.

In such a country-house as that over which Miss Bruce presided, the change to "hunting weather" was greeted with a hearty welcome, but at a few miles' distance it produced no little anxiety and discomfiture. The Roys were about to give a dinner-party, the first

since they came to live at Royston Grange.
They had consulted the almanac, made, as
Nelly said, "a proper arrangement with the
moon," and now, if her light should be obscured
by clouds, if the roads were axle-deep in soft
white mud, if the floods were out, if the rain
came down, if everything conspired to baffle
their guests and spoil their party, husband and
wife agreed "it would be really too provoking."

They were together in the breakfast-room
of Nelly's new home. She locked the tea-
caddy, and fitted its key on a steel ring,
among many others, with a certain house-
wifely care that seemed her second nature; he
paced up and down between window and fire-
place with an impatience that bordered on
disgust.

"If the frost had only lasted over this
confounded dinner-party," said he, "it might
have rained torrents to-morrow and welcome!
I want to get some hunting next week. Now
I wish we hadn't asked the Grantons. She's
delicate—*very*. They'll send an excuse, and

not come—or they'll come and not go away.
If she catches a bad cold, she'll very likely die
in the house!"

"Oh, Mr. Roy!" exclaimed Nelly (she
could not yet bring herself to call her paragon
by so simple a name as John). "She can have
the pink-room, poor dear! It is the warmest
in the house. And I'm sure I'll nurse her
night and day."

"Nonsense, Nelly!" was the marital rejoinder. "I wish I could teach you not to
take everything one says *au pied de la lettre*."

"That's French," she answered good-
humouredly, "but even in French it saves
trouble to say what you mean."

"What I mean is this. If the Grantons
throw us over, you must send all your people
in differently. Are you quite sure you won't
make a mess of the whole thing?"

She pulled a list from her apron-pocket,
written in her own clear, firm hand, and looked
wistfully over its contents.

"I dread that part most of all," she

whispered, with a loving look at him from her deep grey eyes. "The dinner I can superintend well enough, and arranging the furniture, and lighting the company-rooms. It's what I'm used to. But I *am* afraid of the county gentry; and if once I begin wrong, and march them off out of their proper places, I know I shall get as red as a turkey-cock, and think everybody is looking at me. You see I never had to do with great folks, dear, till I knew you."

He bit his lip. How could he be angry with this kind and handsome woman, who loved him so well? Yet it *was* provoking to be obliged to drill her for these little exigencies of every-day life, it *was* tiresome to be always in hot water lest she should say or do something contrary to that unwritten code which it is so impossible to classify or define. Lady Jane would have given him no anxiety on this score. And yet he could not bring himself to wish he had married Lady Jane!

"Remember, dear," he continued kindly

enough, "I take Miss Granton, because she is a Viscount's daughter, and Fitzowen takes you."

"Not Sir Hector Bruce?" said Nelly. "He's a much older man. I was always taught to reverence grey hairs. I wish you had more of them."

"Certainly *not*," he insisted. "Sir Hector is a baronet, and of early creation ; but Fitzowen is an Irish peer——"

"What's an Irish peer?" asked Mrs. Roy. "I shall never take it all in. I thought one lord was as good as another lord, and I still think a baronet of sixty ought to be of more account than a young whipper-snapper not six-and-twenty. But you know best, of course."

"I suppose I do," he answered drily, and deferred for the present his intention of piloting his wife through the intricacies of Debrett.

But while he smoked a cigar in the stable and consulted with his groom on such inexhaustible topics as the grey's fetlock, and the chestnut's cough, he felt that Nelly's ignorance of conventionalities would be a continual source of irritation to his shy and sensitive nature; that notwithstanding her beauty, her sweet temper, her entire devotion to himself, a woman might have suited him better who was more conversant with his own artificial state of society, that he might even have been wiser not to have married at all. It is but justice to add that he had the grace to be ashamed of such reflections, and dismissed them with a jerk, just as he threw away the stump of his cigar.

Half-an-hour later, while bent on her household avocations, he saw her pause as she passed through the conservatory to tie up a pretty little nosegay prepared for his own button-hole when he should go out. Something of the old thrill he felt on the pier at Beachmouth stirred his heart once more. Her attitudes were so graceful, the curves of her figure so true to the line of beauty, her eyes so deep and soft, her features so exquisitely cut, her locks so dark and glossy, he could not but admit that his wife, in appearance at least, was the most bewitching woman he had ever seen.

"As far as looks go," thought John Roy, "she will hold her own with the best, and I can trust .her to be nicely dressed. While dinner lasts it will do well enough, but I know what women are. They'll find her out in the drawing-room, and they'll let her see they've found her out. Nelly will lose her head, and say or do something that will make me feel hot all over. I wish she hadn't asked them! I wish the cook would get drunk, or the kitchen-chimney catch fire, or something frightful would happen to get one out of the whole d——d thing!"

But the cook and the kitchen-chimney remained staunch to their respective duties. Delicate Mrs. Granton did not send an excuse; on the contrary, she was one of the first arrivals, in a remarkably low dress. Sir Hector, Miss Bruce, and Lord Fitzowen, turned up in due course. By eight o'clock the whole party were assembled in the drawing-room. Nelly received them in turn, with exactly the right amount of cordiality, neither too cold nor too gushing, paired them off, and sent them to dinner with a sinking heart indeed, but a perfect imitation of high-bred composure, followed them on Lord Fitzowen's arm with gracious dignity, and Mr. Roy began to breathe freely again.

"After all," he thought, "D'Orsay was right. A good heart is good manners ready made. Nelly couldn't have done it better if she had been born a duke's daughter!"

Soup and fish came and went with the usual soup and fish conversation. Mrs. Granton asked her host how the new stoves answered in his hot-houses, and whether he should take Mrs. Roy to the Hunt ball? The rest told each other that "it was *really* a thaw, that the frost had been enjoyable enough for skaters, that the change was welcome to those who hunt, and—and—Champagne, if you please," after which the talk became more general and more discursive, not without a few agreeable personalities, and remarks, occasionally much to the point. The whole affair seemed to go off smoothly, and though the company were chiefly composed of country neighbours, the entertainment promised to be a success.

People were well paired, and this was the more fortunate, as our table of precedence, regulating English society, leaves nothing to chance. Mrs. Granton, a pleasant little woman, with a tendency to mild flirtation, liked both her host and her neighbour on the other side, a young guardsman, with good spirits, good appetite, and good looks. Two squires, fast friends of thirty years' standing, whose talk was of short-horns, sat together. The venerable clergyman of the parish placed himself next Miss Bruce, a young lady for whom he professed the deepest regard, to which she warmly responded, consulting him on his many charities, and speaking of him in all societies as "a dear old thing!" An unmarried damsel of a certain age, not yet on the retired list, was mated with a veteran admiral, who made up for his weather-worn face and grizzled hair, by that frank and kindly gallantry which women find

so irresistible, and which, combined with hardy
habits and a reputation for personal daring,
renders officers of the Royal Navy such uni-
versal favourites with the sex. Sir Hector,
who sat on the same side of the table as his
daughter, sheltered therefore from the warning
glances with which she was accustomed to
check such imprudences, launched out freely
in the matter of savours and sauces, did not
refuse champagne, and even asked for a glass
of old ale after cheese, though, as Hester
observed, "Papa knew it was poison to him.
Absolutely poison!" Finally, Lord Fitzowen,
who took in his hostess, found himself completely fascinated and enthralled. Her beauty,
her good-humour, above all, her simple manners,
charmed him exceedingly. They were so wholly
different from the artificial graces he was accustomed to in general society.

Fitz, though a gentleman, had, I fear,
promised himself more mirth than interest in
studying the character of John Roy's new
wife. He expected her to furnish amusement

during the evening, food for laughter with
Hester on the morrow, and was surprised to
find how completely he had been mistaken.

Quiet and unobtrusive, she seemed yet to
take her own place as mistress of the house,
with a serene and conscious dignity. While
paying courteous attention to her guests, no
movement of the servants escaped her vigil-
ance. Those deep grey eyes seemed to
observe the requirements of all, and the
training of her early life, the habit of close
attention to trifles, of looking into everything
herself, now stood her in good stead.

Nelly was at high pressure, nevertheless.
She had no fear, indeed, of the cook's failures,
nor of shortcomings on the part of her well-
paid and well-ordered establishment, but she
sadly mistrusted herself.

She had already learned to stand in awe
of her husband's fastidious taste ; she dreaded
at every moment to offend it by something
she might say or do, and she glanced at him
from time to time with an obvious timidity

that was not lost on her sharp-sighted neighbour. "Does he bully her?" thought Fitz.
"She seems afraid of him. She's not quite at
her ease. Good heavens! If I had such a
wife as that, I should worship the very
ground beneath her feet!"

Like many of his class, our friend was an
enthusiast, and at least *believed* himself capable
of romance and self-sacrifice. Some of the
greatest follies on behalf of women have been
perpetrated by men of the world, at whom that
world invariably expresses a well-bred surprise,
wondering they should "not have known
better," ignoring the recklessness that stands
for generosity, and forgetting how its own
treadmil becomes at last so wearisome that
any change is accepted for an improvement.

It is a sad reflection, but, as the practised
angler well knows, to capture fishes of all kinds
there is nothing like a change of bait. So for
the human gudgeon novelty has a keen and
dangerous attraction. A bit of sweet-briar in
the cottager's hedge never seems so fragrant as

after a walk through the duke's conservatories. His Grace himself, when he can get away from his French cook, loves to dine on a simple mutton-chop, and I have always been satisfied that queens and princesses wore the willow for King Cophetua when he placed his crown at the feet of a beggar-maid.

Lord Fitzowen had necessarily been thrown into the society of ladies of high rank—had been refused by the great heiress of one season, smiled on by the great beauty of the next, been a little in love, like everybody else, with the handsomest of duchesses, and had neither lost flesh nor spirits nor appetite from the strength of his attachments. But here was a new experience altogether. Apart from her good looks, he had never met any other woman the least like Mrs. Roy, and he studied her with the feeling of admiration and curiosity that a man experiences who, after a night's sleep on a railway, wakes in the streets of a foreign capital that he has never seen before.

The interest, I must admit, was all on one

side. Nelly seemed much too pre-occupied to think of anything but her female guests—how she was to get them into the drawing-room— what to do with them when there; whether tea and coffee should be served separately or together, once or twice each; and if she ought or ought not to press everybody to stay a little longer after the welcome moment when their carriages were proclaimed to be waiting at the door?

Fitz could see that his attentions left no impression, and this indifference only made him the more desirous of standing well in her good opinion.

"I have been presented to you before to-day, Mrs. Roy," said he, stimulated to exertion by a glass of Chartreuse after ice. "You have forgotten *me*, but I have not forgotten *you*."

"Indeed!" answered Nelly. "It's very stupid of me; I hope you'll excuse it. I was never good at remembering faces."

"You were walking with Roy in the Park. It must have been just before you were married.

I was riding and he introduced me. Do you remember *now* ? "

" I remember your horse ; such a beautiful chestnut. I was always fond of animals. Have you brought it with you to Warden Towers ? "

A little piqued, and feeling rather at a disadvantage, Fitz pulled himself together before answering.

" He is in a stable at the village. I rather agree with you, Mrs. Roy ; I like beasts on four feet better than on two. May I bring him over some day to renew his acquaintance ? "

" Thank you," said Nelly absently. He suspected she had not paid attention to a word. Her faculties were now concentrated on the responsibility of " making the move " to marshal her ladies into the drawing-room. After all she signalled the wrong one, and, observing a cloud on her husband's brows as she passed out, followed the rustling squadron in their retreat with heightened colour and rather a heavy heart.

Lord Fitzowen, though he filled a bumper of Mr. Roy's excellent claret, leaned back in his chair less talkative than usual. His evening's entertainment had not turned out as he expected, and he found himself thinking a good deal more of his friend's wife than his friend's wine.

CHAPTER IX.

STRANGERS YET.

WHEN they had talked enough about poor's-rates, short-horns, the scarcity of foxes, and unpopularity of their Lord-Lieutenant, John Roy sent his brown sherry round for the last time, and suggested coffee in the drawing-room. Entering behind his guests, he stole an eager glance at Nelly, to see how she was getting on.

Yes—it was just as he feared. He had told her particularly to cultivate Mrs. Granton, and there was Mrs. Granton, on a sofa with Miss Bruce, at the far end of the room. The two other ladies of consideration were in close conference over the fire, and his wife sat at a distant table, showing photographs to the mature spinster, who looked more than half asleep.

Roy's anxious, jealous temperament was up in arms on the instant. "D—n it! Nelly," he whispered, over her shoulder, "don't let them send you to Coventry in your own house!" His glance was unkind, and even angry; she had never before heard him swear; with a chill, sick feeling at her heart, she realised, for the first time, how wide a difference there is between marriage and love.

"How can he look at me like that?" thought Nelly, "and at Mrs. Granton as if he could fall down and worship her? If this is good society, I've had enough of it! I wish I had never seen Beachmouth. I wish I had never left Auntie and the hotel. I wish—I wish I was dead and buried, and done with once for all, and he'd got another wife, a *real* lady born, who would suit him better, but could never love him half as well!"

If anybody had said a kind word to her she must have burst out crying, but the servants were moving about with tea and coffee, there was an adjournment to the card-tables, and by the time eight of the party had settled to whist, and two to *bézique,* she recovered her equanimity, feeling only unreasonably tired and depressed.

Nelly disliked cards. Lord Fitzowen had "cut out" at the nearest whist table. I will not take upon me to say that he was disappointed when he found his hostess the only other unoccupied person in the room.

A pianoforte stood near the door into the conservatory, which was well lighted, and looked very pretty with its exotics, rock-work, and fountain in the midst. He asked her to play, and Nelly was too shy to refuse, but her courage failed when she sat down, so they opened music-books, and talked about them instead.

John Roy, sorting a handful of trumps, turned round to see that his guests were amused. "If you like to smoke, Fitzowen," said he, "nobody minds it in the conservatory —only shut the glass door. Take him, Nelly, and show him how."

Lord Fitzowen, thus invited, professed great eagerness to see the conservatory, and was careful to close the door of communication with the drawing-room, though nothing would induce him to light a cigar in the presence of his hostess.

So they walked up and down inhaling the heavy perfume of hot-house flowers, reading their Latin names, and hanging over the gold fish in their basin under the fountain. Finally, they seated themselves at the extreme end, and Mrs. Roy, who felt she ought to say something, observed, " It was very quiet and pleasant, after the heat in the other rooms. She often brought her work here, and sat listening to the fountain, till she fancied she was miles and miles away."

Fitzowen glanced sharply in her face. No, she was not speaking for effect, and seemed simply to state a fact that led to nothing more. She looked as if she was thinking, deeply too, but of what—of whom ? She baffled him, she puzzled him. This was the most interesting woman he ever met in his life !

He had penetration enough to see that she

was shy, and ill at ease. Diffident people have usually a keen sense of the ludicrous. If he could make her laugh, she would feel more at home with him, and he might hope to obtain her goodwill and friendship—perhaps,. in time, her confidence and regard.

"I quite agree with you, Mrs. Roy," said he, "I have the same sensations myself; all this wealth of green vegetables seems to raise me into another phase of existence. I feel like a caterpillar, for instance, in a cabbage-leaf, or a sweep on May-day."

"I don't know about the caterpillar," she answered, with rather a sad smile. "But I dare say the sweeps are very happy on May-day. I often think that you great people, who do nothing but amuse yourselves, are not half so contented as those who work for their bread."

"Every man to his trade, Mrs. Roy. I couldn't earn a shilling a day at any employment you can name. I was brought up to amuse myself."

"And I to work. Yes, you may laugh;

but I was taught from a child to gain an honest livelihood. I'm not ashamed of it. I wouldn't change places with one of those ladies in the next room. Only, I sometimes wish Mr. Roy had been a poor man. He would have felt how hard I tried to make him comfortable."

"He does *not* feel it now," thought Lord Fitzowen—"and this is another of the many wives who consider themselves unappreciated and misunderstood;" but he was too discreet to put his sentiments into words, and only answered by a look of sympathy and expectation.

She remained silent for a minute, then broke off a sprig of geranium, and continued, more to herself than her companion,—

"I wonder if people get on better for being exactly alike in character, or in all respects different. I often puzzle over it for hours when I'm sitting here listening to the drip of the fountain, and watching the gold fish. I dare say they're sometimes unhappy too, poor things!"

"Fish are *always* discontented," he answered gravely. "But with regard to the previous question. I am convinced that husbands and wives ought to be as different as—as—chalk from cheese. The man is the chalk, of course, · and the woman the cheese."

"I'm glad to hear you say that," replied Mrs. Roy. "Only, perhaps you are not the best judge, being a bachelor."

"How do you know I'm a bachelor?"

She blushed in some trepidation, lest she should have stumbled into another solecism.

"I beg your pardon," she faltered. "I—I was not aware. I had not heard of your being married. I hope I have said nothing wrong."

He laughed merrily. "Don't be alarmed, Mrs. Roy. I am still a beast untamed, a gentleman at large, a virgin page, whatever you choose to call it. When my time *does* come, I hope the lady will be most unlike myself!"

"I dare say she will be very nice," observed Nelly simply. "But, whatever you do, Lord

Fitzowen, don't marry a woman below your rank in life ; partly for your own sake, but a great deal more for hers !"

His tone was much graver, and he looked in the face of his hostess with an expression of sincere respect and regard, while he answered,—

"Pardon me, Mrs. Roy. There I cannot agree with you. A man is seldom fortunate enough to marry his ideal, but, at least, he should try. Shall I tell you mine ? A woman of character, a woman of energy—not afraid to take her part in the business of life, nor ashamed to acknowledge it; despising only what is base, and hating only what is wrong. The less she knows of that artificial game we call society, with its unworthy interests and petty artifices, the better. Frank, natural, and simple, I should like her all the more for utter ignorance of the great world, and a complete indifference to its ways. Now I've told you my notion of a wife, Mrs. Roy. Of course she must be handsome, and have black hair like yours—but that has nothing to do with it."

Her heart beat faster. He had described a character the very counterpart of her own, and he was an acknowledged judge of human nature, a thorough man of the world, occupying even a higher position than her own husband. Perhaps she had deceived herself, after all, and magnified mole-hills into mountains, from sheer anxiety lest she should fall short of the standard required by that paragon. She looked in Fitzowen's frank, handsome face, and felt that here was a friend in whom she could confide, a counsellor on whom she could rely. Versed in worldly ways, but untainted by worldly duplicty; wise, good-natured, and experienced, he would point out the path to follow, the difficulties to be avoided; in a word, would teach her to retain her hold on the affections of Mr. Roy.

She pulled to pieces the bit of geranium in her hand, as if absorbed in that occupation, but stole an anxious look at him from under her long eyelashes the while.

"You—you are an old friend of my husband's, are you not?" she asked in a low, uncertain voice.

He had a scale of friendship, regulated on a tariff of his own. "I would lend him a fiver," he thought, "if he wanted it; perhaps a pony. Certainly not a monkey." But though there is a wide margin between twenty-five pounds and five hundred, he felt justified in answering, "Yes, a very old friend," bravely enough.

"Lord Fitzowen," she continued. "If I tell you something in confidence, will you promise not to repeat it to a soul?"

"Honour among thieves, Mrs. Roy. You and I are not thieves, and you may trust me as you would your solicitor!"

"I would rather trust you as my husband's friend, and I will. You know, or perhaps you do *not* know, that till we married I never lived among the sort of people I meet now every day. I was respectably brought up, and well-educated, Lord Fitzowen, but my father was a trades-man, and my mother a governess. I am not ashamed of them, far from it, only in such a station it was not to be expected, of course, that I could acquire the manners and habits of the class I have to mix with now. I try to learn day by day, but it is such uphill work, and I have nobody to teach me!"

"They had much better learn of *you*. I beg pardon for interrupting!"

"If I ask Mr. Roy, he is vexed, and I cannot bear to see him cross. He seems to expect one to know things by instinct. I am dreadfully put about by little difficulties that you would think the merest trifles. But they are no trifles to *me!* It's like not knowing how to spell a word when you write a letter, and having no dictionary."

"Shall I be your dictionary?"

"Will you? It's what I wanted to ask, only I didn't quite know how. It would be a great relief, for sometimes, I do assure you, I feel at my wits' end. Now I will consult *you*, if you don't mind."

"Mind! I would do anything in the world for you—and for him."

"Thank you, Lord Fitzowen. Don't think me ungrateful because I say little about it. I feel your kindness deeply all the same. Now we'll go back to the drawing-room. The whist-players will be wondering what can have kept us so long."

"One moment, Mrs. Roy. Have you any reason to believe there's a ghost somewhere loose about the garden?"

"A ghost! Good gracious. Why?"

"Simply, that for the last ten minutes I have seen a pale, unearthly face pressed against the glass, glaring at us from outside. Square, flat, hard-featured, and not a pretty face by any means."

Nelly's spirits were rising. "Square, flat, hard-featured," she repeated with a laugh, "and not a pretty face by any means. Oh! then I shouldn't wonder if it was Mrs. Mopus!"

CHAPTER X.

MRS. MOPUS.

"Who is Mrs. Mopus?" but there came no answer to his question, for already the rubbers had been lost and won; the carriages were announced. A table was set out with brandy, seltzer, ice, lemons, and cold water, the modern substitute for stirrup-cups of former days; and Lord Fitzowen's hostess was too much engrossed with the ceremonies of leave-taking to spare him any further attention. Nevertheless, when it came to his turn to wish her good-night, she gave him her hand with such marked cordiality, as to excite the observation even of Mr. Roy.

"How do you like our friend Fitz, Nelly?" asked her husband, yawning his way upstairs. "You had every opportunity to-night of forming an opinion."

"I think him very nice," answered Nelly, with a bright smile.

"Most women do," he replied drily, and shut his door.

Almost at the same moment, in the obscurity of a closed landau, Miss Bruce asked Lord Fitzowen the same question about Mrs. Roy. Fitz did not respond quite so frankly.

"Wants knowing, I should say," was his verdict. "Very quiet, very reserved. A character like my own, I think. Born to blush unseen; and bloom brightest in the shade."

"You ought to blush unseen in that corner," laughed Hester, "for being such a humbug! If you're both so shy and reserved, Lord Fitz, perhaps you will tell me what you found to talk about for a good hour in the conservatory?"

But Lord Fitz made no answer. He was still ruminating on the last question he asked his hostess, "Who is Mrs. Mopus?"

Mrs. Mopus was neither more nor less than the housekeeper at Royston Grange, and in that capacity regarded John Roy's new wife with no small amount of jealousy and ill-will. So long as her master remained a bachelor, visiting his home, at long intervals, to bring with him a houseful of bachelors like himself, with their valets, she found the selection exceedingly to her taste. In his absence, she was an independent sovereign ; when he came back, a lady patroness, presiding over an agreeable little circle of gentlemen's gentlemen, with whom her word was law, particularly at supper-time.

She had great opportunities for peculation, of which she availed herself moderately, but with scrupulous regularity ; could engage or discharge housemaids, laundry-maids, and kitchen-maids at will, won a series of triumphs over the successive cooks who came and went like the slides of a magic-lantern ; and after a protracted contest with the Scotch gardener, found herself unquestioned mistress of Royston Grange.

She was a widow, with one good-for-nothing

son, alive or dead in Australia, of whom she possessed no other memento than an ill-looking photograph. Energetic, resolute, and persevering, had she been ten years younger, she would surely have tried to marry Mr. Roy; but the looking-glass told her such a scheme was hopeless, and she gave it up almost as soon as it crossed her mind.

When she learned he was going to take a wife, she respectfully tendered her resignation, knowing well it would not be accepted. John Roy (so like a man!), hating all trouble of a domestic nature, begged her, of course, to remain, and for a time she speculated on the chance of his bride being a young, inexperienced woman, whom with her cunning and audacity she might turn round her finger like the rest of the household. It was a serious blow to discover that the new Mrs. Roy seemed as practised an adept in the science of house-keeping as herself, knowing the due consumption of butcher's meat to a pound, of coals and sugar to a lump, that she would no more submit to stealthy pilfering than to open robbery, and was resolved, in accordance with one of the first instincts of womanhood, to be mistress in her own house.

Mrs. Mopus did not yield without a struggle, but in the very first trial of strength found herself so ignobly defeated, less by Nelly's quiet dignity of manner than her intimate knowledge of the subject in question (a supply of sandpaper and soap for the housemaid's closet), that she determined in future to avoid coming to conclusions with her new mistress, preferring rather to watch and wait till opportunity offered, and then do her the worst turn that lay in her power.

She had no little knowledge of the world and its ways. John Roy, who took her from a recommendation, and not a character, was quite satisfied with her own account of how the intervening time—some seven or eight years—had been spent since she left her last situation. She professed to have been in business as a fancy stationer, and to have failed—of course through the rascality of an agent; but the valet of one of Mr. Roy's shooting friends could have told him a different story. She had been keeping a small public-house of no good repute near Croydon, which this worthy frequented when attending certain suburban steeplechases, where he was in the habit of wagering freely with his late master's money. He prided himself, however, on being no less a man of honour than a man of the world, and gave her to understand, doubtless for some practical equivalent, that he had no intention of showing her up. Still, she felt that her position was insecure, her tenure uncertain—more so than ever since the arrival of Mrs. Roy, and she cherished for her new mistress that good-will which animates the bosom of one woman for another who has thwarted, supplanted, and found her out.

After their supper in "the room," as it was called—an elaborate meal, of which every upper servant felt bound in honour to promote the hilarity and comfort—Mrs. Mopus had con-

tracted a habit of walking out of doors for
half-an-hour or so in all weathers and under
all circumstances, protesting that she could not
get to sleep without this taste of fresh air after
the labours of the day. Her real reasons were,
perhaps, not entirely sanitary. It might be
convenient thus to withdraw for a stated portion
of time daily from the observation of the household, and no questions asked! When first she
established the practice she was narrowly
watched, no doubt, by her fellow-servants, but
in the course of a few months, when nothing
came of these nightly wanderings, they ceased
to regard them, and Mrs. Mopus found herself
free to steal about the gardens and shrubberies
wherever she pleased, unnoticed in the dark.

It was thus she held private interviews
with the butcher to accommodate certain serious
differences concerning the heavy overcharges
on which he tried to put her off with a shabby
ten per cent., and it was thus, too, that she
clandestinely met a neighbouring farmer, sixty
years of age and given to inebriety, who made

honourable proposals of marriage, broken off prematurely by his being sold-up on quarter-day.

When there was company at Royston Grange, it was her habit in these nightly prowlings to peer through its panes into the conservatory. It amused her to watch the young men who adjourned there for coffee and tobacco, moving about among the flowers, like tropical birds, in their gorgeous smoking-costumes. She was edified, too, by the freedom of their conversation, picking up occasional scraps of scandal, concerning great people in London, or country neighbours nearer home, of which she would otherwise have remained ignorant. Collating their version of such affairs with that of their valets, she formed her own conclusions, and revolved them in her mind for future use. It was one of her maxims that the knowledge of a fellow-creature's secret (for evil) was as good as a bank-note. The time was sure to come when either he would pay to keep it quiet, or somebody else to find it out.

But her observations had hitherto been confined to the male sex. It seemed a great piece of luck to detect, on this night of the dinner-party, a lady sitting alone with a gentleman in the conservatory ; a greater, to discover that lady was Mrs. Roy. Their conversation, indeed, might have been published in the first column of the *Times ;* but there is no dialogue so innocent that it will not bear misconstruction, and the listening housekeeper overheard enough to lay the foundation of such a plot as she hoped would undermine the life's happiness of her mistress, estrange her from her husband, and drive her at last ignominiously from her home. If she had any scruples of pity, they were blown into air by Nelly's last remark while she entered the drawing-room—" Not a pretty face, by any means. Oh ! then I shouldn't wonder if it was Mrs. Mopus ! "

" And Mrs. Mopus will be even with you yet, before she's done ! " muttered the housekeeper, as she crept back through the laurels, shaking with suppressed passion. " What are *you*, my fine lady, I should like to know, for all your stylish looks and your black hair? Why, you're no better born than myself, and no better brought up! If you'd been a real lady, a lady of quality, you'd have kept your own place in the drawing-room, *like* a lady, and not come poking your nose into the linen-closets and the store-room with me. Lady, indeed! If that young gentleman, and he *is* a gentleman, and a lord into the bargain, knew what I do, he wouldn't be so keen to follow up and down, like a dog at your heels. And Mr. Roy, too, I'd like to hear what he would say to such goings on. He shall know them, too, that he shall, before he's twenty-four hours older. I've been a faithful servant to him and his for many a long year, and I'm not going to see him put upon now. Not a pretty face, and you wouldn't wonder if it was Mrs. Mopus! Yes, it *is* Mrs. Mopus, and that you shall find out, my fine madam, to your cost!"

She was so angry that she went straight to her bed-room, and sat by the light of a single tallow-candle, cogitating her plans far into the night.

Mrs. Roy, meanwhile, unconscious of coming evil, congratulated herself on the success of her dinner-party, and her own observance of those formalities she had so dreaded for more than a week.

"I never made a single mistake, did I?" she asked next morning at breakfast, peeping triumphantly round the tea-urn at her husband.

"Not many," he answered. "You made the move after dinner to the rector's wife instead of Mrs. Granton, and you didn't half take notice of that tiresome old Lady Meadow-bank."

Nelly's face fell. "I'm so sorry, dear," said she. "It's nice of you to want to be kind to her, poor woman, for she's a widow."

"Oh! it's not for that," he answered sharply. "You never seem to understand things, Nelly. She owns the best Covert in the country."

Mrs. Roy looked rather sad, and held her tongue.

A few such conjugal amenities, a few lectures on the proprieties from Mr. Roy, followed by silent tears, the bitterer that she was heartily ashamed of them, and Nelly began to lose confidence in herself, to dread the very tingle of the door-bell that announced visitors, and to make more conventional mistakes than ever in sheer nervousness, and anxiety lest she should do wrong.

If, as has been said, the great secret of oratory is to entertain a thorough contempt for one's audience, so the art of shining in society cannot be successfully cultivated under feelings of diffidence, and mistrust of one's own position or one's own powers. Mrs. Roy would glance anxiously at her husband before she spoke, say the wrong thing when she *did* speak, or stop short in the middle of a sentence, as if conscious of her blunders, and waiting his instructions to go on—then he would shoot angry glances at her, which 'made matters worse; and once, after a certain luncheon to which some neighbours arrived unexpectedly, he reproached her for her awkwardness, her timidity, above all her silence, and told her— positively told her—" he couldn't bear to see her sitting at the top of his table, mum like a fool!"

The last feather fairly broke the back of her self-respect. She began to long for sympathy, for help, instruction, and advice. If Lord Fitzowen would only come, she thought he might tell her what to do; he was so kind, so considerate, so ready to share with her his experience and knowledge of the world. That very afternoon Lord Fitzowen *did* come. She saw him ride past the windows while she was sitting disconsolately at tea, and ran to the glass before he was announced, to smoothe her hair, and make sure her eyes did not look as if she had been crying.

John Roy, marking trees for thinning, met his visitor in the park. " I'd come back with you," said he, wiping his bill-hook on the hedger's gloves he wore, " only I've got so wet amongst all this underwood. But go up to the house; you'll find Nelly at home. She'll be glad to see you; she's rather in the dumps, it will do her good." And he returned to that most engrossing of all occupations, chopping in one's own plantations, while Lord Fitzowen cantered over the grass to pass his visit of ceremony to Mrs. Roy.

CHAPTER XI.

SHE received him with a bright smile, that faded to a look of womanly concern when he gave her his left hand.

"Why, you've got your arm in a sling," said she. "What is it? Nothing serious, I hope. You've had a tumble from your horse."

John Roy would have told her she used the wrong expression. A good rider *falls with* his horse, a bad one *tumbles off*. Fitzowen answered carelessly, "It serves me right for hunting before the frost was quite gone. I've put my shoulder out. It's nothing to signify, and luckily I didn't hurt your friend, the chestnut."

"If you had not hurt yourself it would be more to the purpose. Did you ride him here?"

"How could I, Mrs. Roy? He was out hunting yesterday. No. I came over on one of Miss Bruce's ponies."

She jumped to conclusions like a very woman. Of course! she ought to have seen it long ago. How stupid she had been! Mr. Roy was quite right when he said she was not fit to find her way about in general society. Miss Bruce and this young nobleman were lovers, and in all probability engaged. She might confide in Lord Fitzowen now without the slightest reserve or afterthought. It was fortunate—providential; and yet she could not help reflecting that Hester seemed unlike the sort of person he had described as his ideal of a wife.

"I see," she observed after a pause. "Of course you would."

"What do you see?" he asked; "and of course I would what?"

"Of course you will have some tea. Shall I make it for you? Not so well as Miss Bruce, but the best I can."

"I didn't come here to talk about Miss Bruce," said he, subsiding into a low chair while she handed him his tea. "I am more interested at this moment in Mrs. Roy. Has she had many visitors? Has she given any more dinner-parties? And what has become of the ghost?"

"The ghost?"

"Yes. Don't you remember the ghost I saw looking into the conservatory?"

"Do you believe in ghosts?"

"Implicitly."

"And in spirit-rapping?"

"I think so, though they never come to rap at *my* door. I believe in everything, Mrs. Roy. That is to say, I believe in one thing as much as another."

She looked grave.

"I don't like to hear you speak so, and you don't mean it, I know. Lord Fitzowen, do you remember what I told you the other night about the ways of society? I cannot understand them. Have people no likings, no

affections, no feelings, above all, no standard
of right and wrong? or do they simply make a
point of *never* saying what they mean? You
have lived in the great world; you belong to it
yourself. Perhaps you will explain."

"I will if I can," he answered. "You
know I promised to be your dictionary."

"It was kind of you, if you *meant* it. I
have thought so very often. I do indeed
require a dictionary more than most people."

"Then being yours, I shall at once turn
over a new leaf."

"Most men in your position ought to do
that," she answered, still thinking of Miss
Bruce. "But will you be serious for a
moment, if I ask you a question?"

"To please *you*, I will. For no other consideration on earth."

"Then tell me why it is that only poor
people and servants are ever in earnest about
anything. Mr. Roy is as bad as the others.
You are all alike, and it seems to me you don't
speak English. If it pours with rain, you call

it 'moistish;' if the sun shines, you admit 'it's
not half a bad day.' When young Mr. Slow-
man's horse ran away, and I said it was a
great mercy he wasn't killed, Mrs. Granton
added, 'and a great pity, too,' and all the company laughed. The Browns have lost every
shilling they possessed, but Mr. Roy only
thinks 'it's rather a bore for Brown!' Even
when that horrid woman left her husband the
other day, and it got into all the newspapers,
nobody seemed to consider the wickedness, but
everybody exclaimed, 'How could she be such
a fool!' Are you really without heart and
principles, or do you think it good manners to
appear so?"

"There is affectation in every class, Mrs.
Roy," answered Fitz, plunging boldly into the
question, as knowing he must soon be out of
his depth; "and all affectation is vulgarity
more or less. In our horror of one extreme,
we fall into the other; and for fear we should
seem dramatic, we cease to be real. So we are
vulgar, too, in our way. And yet what would

you have? It would never do for us to go about proclaiming our likes and dislikes—our hopes, feelings, and opinions. We should be ridiculous; worse than that—tiresome. So we agree to play with counters instead of money, and it comes to the same thing when you are used to the game. Why, if I was to tell you what I am really thinking at this moment, how do I know you wouldn't ring the bell and have me turned out of the house?"

She drew herself up, and looked quite capable of acting precisely as he described; but before her pride could take offence, he rattled on into smooth water again.

"I don't care—I'll risk it with *you*, and run my chance. I was thinking what a flat my friend Roy is to be working like a slave up to his middle in dripping underwood when he might be sitting warm and dry by this comfortable fire in the best of company, over an excellent cup of tea. You haven't rung the bell yet, so I would go on, only I have nothing more to say."

" You have said quite enough," she answered laughing, " when you presume to call Mr. Roy ' a flat.' But he never takes tea now, as he used ; and gentlemen seem to find a charm that is perfectly unaccountable in chopping their own trees."

" I am so glad I never had any trees. Not that it matters, for I suppose I should have cut them all down. But you are making me forget everything it is my duty to remember. Now what do you think brought me here this after-noon ? "

Nobody so good-looking as Nelly could be less of a coquette. Still it was not in woman's nature to suppress the obvious rejoinder—

" I suppose it was in order to pay *me* a visit."

" Not a bit. You like people to be rude and sincere, so now I will tell you the truth. I made it *an excuse* to pay you a visit, that I freely admit, but I came charged with a mes-sage from Miss Bruce. The hounds meet to-morrow three miles from this house. She is not going to ride, and would call for you in the carriage if you choose to come. It is a favourite place, and I think I can promise you will be amused."

Nelly's grey eyes sparkled. "I should like it of all things," she answered. "Do you know I have never seen a hunt in my life? Only I'm afraid it's cruel," she added as an afterthought.

"You must not say, 'seeing a hunt.' Your dictionary tells you to call it 'going out hunting;' and as for being cruel, it's, it's—in fact, it's quite the reverse. Then I may tell Miss Bruce you will drive with her?"

"I must ask Mr. Roy. I will, most certainly, if he has no objection."

"What objection *could* he have? I suppose he's not afraid to trust you with Miss Bruce."

"If *you* are not, I don't see why *he* should be," answered Nelly, still harping on her own erroneous conclusion.

He looked mystified, but proceeded to the practical details of their expedition.

" Then she will be at your door at half-past ten. Don't ask her to get out, because she will be wrapped up for all day ; and if you take my advice, you will put on your warmest clothes too. It's sure to be cold crossing the downs. You must go by the old Roman Road. I dare say you don't know the shortest way out of your own woods. Where's the Ordnance Map ? I can show you in five seconds."

Now the Ordnance Map, notwithstanding that it was referred to three or four times every day, hung, for greater convenience, in the most remote corner of the library ; so Mrs. Roy and her visitor adjourned there forthwith ; the latter, as his hostess piloted him across the darkening hall, professing grave apprehensions lest they should meet the ghost !

It was already dusk. John Roy, in his wet clothes, made the best of his way home, following a narrow path through some thick-growing evergreens that led direct to the house. Here he came into collision with an advancing form, shadowy and indistinct enough, but far too substantial in its proportions for a disembodied spirit of any kind.

On one side a scream was suppressed, on the other an oath was *not;* but Mrs. Mopus, perhaps because she expected him, recognised her master before the familiar voice broke out with—

"Who the devil are *you?* And what are you doing here?"

"It's only *me*, sir," she answered softly. "I thought you would be coming home this way, and I slipped out to meet you, Mr. Roy; that's the truth. It's right that somebody should be careful of your health, you that never thinks of yourself. I said you'd be as wet as a sop, and so you are; but you wouldn't go and change, not if it was ever so, unless I begged and prayed it of you, as I always used. I've done my duty by you, Mr. Roy, for a many years, and I'll do it still; whether others does or doesn't, it won't alter me."

"I believe you have a regard for me, Mopus," he answered kindly. "But you are always over-anxious, and make a fuss about nothing."

"Old servants will, sir," she replied. "We know when we've got a good master, Mr. Roy. I've laid down dry things to air at your dressing-room fire, sir. That valet of yours is no more use than a post. No doubt Mrs. Roy would have seen to it herself, but she's engaged in the drawing-room with a visitor."

"Is he not gone *yet?*" escaped from John Roy's lips, with an involuntary expression of surprise.

"I don't know, I'm sure," answered the housekeeper. "It's no business of mine, sir, to watch the gentlemen as comes to visit your lady. I keep to my place, I hope, Mr. Roy, though, of course, my thoughts are my own."

"Thoughts! What do you mean by your thoughts?"

"Well, sir, you mustn't pay much attention to what I say; I'm a little upset this afternoon with one thing and another, and I can't forget you've been a kind master to me for many a

long day.   Get into the house, sir, as quick as
you can, and change from head to foot."

Now the shortest way into the house was
by the drawing-room windows, of which the
shutters had not yet been closed for the night;
and past these windows Mrs. Mopus thought
well to follow in her master's wake, though her
own dominions lay in another wing.   Suddenly
she came alongside, and addressed him in a
troubled whisper.   "I ask your pardon," said
she—"I've deceived you, sir, regarding the
gentleman who came to visit Mrs. Roy.   He
must be gone long ago.   See, there's nobody
left in the drawing-room, and the fire is nearly
out."

"All right, Mopus," he answered, shutting
the house-door; but he muttered to himself as
he tramped up-stairs, "That woman must be
going out of her senses.   What can it signify
to *me* whether there's anybody in the drawing-
room or not?"

Nevertheless, during the process of undress-
ing, her words and manner recurred to him

more than once, always with increasing uneasiness and a vague feeling of suspicion.

Did she mean anything? *If* she meant
anything, why couldn't she speak out? Was
there anything to mean? Anything wrong
going on in the household that he ought to
know? She seemed to imply as much. No
doubt it would come out in good time—to-
morrow or next day. He need not worry
himself. Nelly would see to it, and put everything right. Then he started in his slippers,
and rushed to the window. The clatter of
hoofs could be heard from the stable-yard, and
Fitzowen's good-humoured voice conversing
with the helper who led his pony out.

For one moment the room seemed to turn
round, the next, he muttered, "It's impossible!"
and resumed his dressing calmly and method-
ically as before. But the "it" was not so
easily shaken off; and after attending him
through the successive stages of his toilet,
accompanied him down-stairs to assist at a *tête-
à-tête* dinner with his wife.

Nelly was brilliant, and seemed in better spirits than usual. She looked forward with pleasure to her expedition on the morrow, and felt gratified by Lord Fitzowen's kindness in coming to suggest it to-day. John Roy, on the other hand, ate little and spoke less; but, contrary to his usual habits, which were strictly temperate, drank two or three glasses of wine in quick succession.

It is one of the drawbacks to matrimony, that two people are seldom precisely in the same humour, at the same time. Should the husband be helped twice to mutton, the wife is pretty sure to send her plate away untouched. If *he* is inclined to talk, *she* probably has a headache, and the lady is prone to broach subjects involving personal discussion when the gentleman wants to go to sleep. While the servants were in the room, Nelly did her best, but it is hard to keep the shuttlecock of conversation going with only one battledore, and, as she originated topic after topic, they fell successively to the ground. At last, when dessert was placed on the table, and the door shut for the last time, she made a great effort, and asked her husband, point-blank, "What was the matter?"

"Why?"

It was a discouraging reply, and she continued timidly—

"You seem out of spirits, dear, and you scarcely ate a morsel. Either you didn't like your dinner, or else you're not well."

"The dinner was no worse than usual," he answered ungraciously; "and I don't see why you should say I'm not well, because I can't jabber about nothing, with three servants in the room. A man needn't ask his wife to excuse him, I suppose, whenever he feels tired?"

"Or cross," she replied hastily, for his tone cut her to the quick.

"Or bored," was the unkind rejoinder. "I think that's nearer the mark!"

Her eyes filled with tears, and after five minutes of painful silence she left the room.

But in less than half an hour her sweet and

generous temper re-asserted itself. When tea came she gave him his cup with as bright a smile as usual, drew his arm-chair to the fire, and handed him the newspaper as if no cloud had ever come between them. Even bent her beautiful head over him to whisper softly that she "had spoken in haste, and begged his pardon, because she was in the wrong."

John Roy's heart smote him, and for a moment he esteemed her as "excellent a wench" as ever Othello thought Desdemona: but again there came between them the vague and un-acknowledged shadow cast by the inexplicable bearing of his housekeeper, and he could not refrain from asking himself over and over again, though not without a certain bitter self-con-tempt, "What *could* Mrs. Mopus mean?"

CHAPTER XII.

BURTON BRAKE.

"Not going to ride!" exclaimed Miss Bruce, who was presiding over half-a-dozen guests at the breakfast-table, as Lord Fitzowen appeared in his usual morning dress, with one arm still disabled and in a sling. "I thought your shoulder was better; this *is* a disappointment. Consider, Lord Fitz, your new friend Mrs. Roy won't see you in a red coat."

"Don't hit a fellow when he's down, Miss Bruce," answered his lordship, walking to a well-covered side-table. "I'm hardly man enough to ride my brown horse with both hands; he would have it all his own way if I tried to steer him with one. No; if you'll have me, I'm going to drive with *you*."

"I understand!" replied Hester. "Yes,

you shall come with us if you feel equal to taking care of two ladies. It's very touching, I must say, when I think of all you are giving up. Burton Brake's the only good place on that side of our country."

" I would give up anything for the pleasure of driving with *you*, Miss Bruce."

" And Mrs. Roy, Lord Fitz. Your memory is very short, you seem to have forgotten Mrs. Roy."

" John Roy's new wife !" exclaimed one of the red-coats, stretching a scarlet arm out for toast. " Is *she* going with you, Miss Bruce ? They tell me she is as handsome as paint ; but nobody knows where she came from. Wasn't she an actress, or a shop-woman, or something ?"

" Ask Lord Fitzowen," said Hester.

" Actress ! shop-woman ! Nothing of the kind," replied that nobleman, provoked to feel, for the first time since he left Eton, as if he was going to blush. " She is as ladylike a person as ever you saw. Amiable, accomplished,

well-mannered, and—and—that's all I know
about her."

It seemed a lame conclusion, provoking
general laughter, during which the carriage
was announced, and as a couple of hacks had
been trampling the gravel before the windows
for the last ten minutes, it was voted time to
be off.

So early a start did not seem necessary
from Royston Grange, which was some miles
nearer the place of meeting. Its master could
therefore enjoy two rather unusual luxuries on
a hunting morning, a leisurely toilet and an
unhurried breakfast. In his red coat, white
leathers, top-boots, and bright spurs, all well-
cleaned and well put on, John Roy looked no
unfavourable specimen of the English gentleman, and we may be sure Nelly thought so
too. She had not yet seen him often enough
in this striking attire, for the admiration, mixed
with wonder, which it produced to have palled
on her unaccustomed eyes, though she was less
impressed than a certain damsel totally unused

to the society of sportsmen who married a
friend of my own many years ago.

If this lady ever heard of fox-hunting, she
had no idea that any special dress was required
for that amusement. Hitherto she had only
seen a scarlet coat on the back of a British
soldier or a royal footman. Language is
powerless to convey her feeling of terror and
dismay when in the third week of their honey-
moon, on the first Monday in November, her
husband came down to breakfast gorgeous from
head to foot in full hunting costume.

She felt she was bound for life to a mad-
man; an illusion that the experience of many
succeeding Novembers failed entirely to dispel.

"I like you so much in your red coat," said
Nelly, with her frank bright smile, as Mr. Roy,
moving more stiffly than usual, took his place
at the breakfast-table. "Only I wish, I *do*
wish hunting was not so dangerous!" Every
man in his heart would be thought "prodigal
of his person," but he was too honest not to
admit, though he went straight enough when

the hounds ran, that with good horses, well-ridden, he reduced the risk of crossing a country to a minimum.

"Wait till you've been out and seen us ride, Nelly," he answered pleasantly, "you'll never think it dangerous again."

Last night's ill-humour had vanished; coming clouds were as yet below the horizon. He felt in high spirits, anticipating no little enjoyment from the day's sport. If he was pleased, *she* was happy, and while she pinned a hot-house flower in his button-hole and gave him a parting kiss, she felt as if the old days had come back once more. The old days! how old were they, after all? She could count the intervening time by weeks, and yet there seemed a break, a gap, a gulf between then and now.

As his distance from the meet was but three miles, Mr. Roy rode from the door on the hunter he intended to keep out all day. Nelly watched man and horse till they disappeared with a swelling heart. How she admired her husband, how she loved him! Surely she had everything she wanted in the world—what was this vague misgiving? this shadowy foreboding of evil, that haunted her at every turn?

There was no time for such speculations. Already an open carriage might be seen bowling along the avenue, and Mrs. Roy, with innate good-breeding, flew up-stairs to put on her things, that she might not keep Hester waiting at the door.

It was no unpleasant surprise to find Lord Fitzowen, buttoned up in an Ulster coat, occupying the front seat of the barouche. With her usual frankness, Nelly told him so, and wondered why Miss Bruce should look more amused, and his lordship more pleased, than the occasion seemed to warrant.

But she had never been out hunting before, even on wheels, and all other feelings were soon lost in the novelty and excitement of the situation.

"It was like taking a child about," said Hester describing their drive the same afternoon to Sir Hester at tea. "I mean to be fonder of Mrs. Roy than anybody in the county. She *is* a dear thing, Papa, so fresh, so honest, and so charmingly unsophisticated! When we overtook the hounds in the Fosse Road, she actually clapped her hands with delight. We couldn't help laughing, and she *did* look perfectly beautiful when she blushed. I am sure Lord Fitz thought so too!"

Miss Bruce was right, his lordship enjoyed his day's hunting even more than his companions, though it must be confessed that some of Mrs. Roy's questions on the noble science puzzled him exceedingly.

Like most ladies, she seemed interested in riding rather than hunting, in horses rather than hounds. It was no easy matter to satisfy her shrewd and inquiring mind, as to the powers of a good hunter, and what fences should or should *not* be attempted in the hurry of the chase. Did not Mr. Roy's bodily safety depend on the solution of such problems?

Pointing to some strong ash rails nearly five feet high, with a wide ditch on the landing side into the road, along which they were driving—"Could your horse leap *that*, Lord Fitzowen," she asked; "or would it be impossible? I hope it would!"

He felt constrained to admit, however forbidding this obstacle might appear, there were many good hunters that, properly ridden, could clear it without a mistake.

"Then if you came to it, you would go over, of course?" she continued, looking anxiously in his face.

Hester's mirthful eyes were on him, and he was obliged to tell the truth.

"I would rather go round by Warden Towers," said he. "I would rather lose the best run that ever was seen. I would rather never go out hunting again!"

"But why, if it's not impossible?"

"Why? Mrs. Roy. Why? Well, I suppose, because I am afraid!"

She looked immensely relieved, and seemed

able now to turn her attention with unalloyed enjoyment to the business of the hour.

This commenced from the moment they arrived at the place of meeting. Such of the county gentlemen as had not yet been introduced, reined · in their horses and made their bows, as gracefully as bridles and hat-strings would permit. Miss Bruce was a general favourite, but her companion seemed, to-day, the centre of attraction; and many glances of unqualified admiration, from sports-men of all ages and sizes, were launched at the open carriage where sat "Roy's new wife."

She looked about for her husband in vain. He came by a shorter way than the party in the carriage, and, as he rode slowly, arrived only when the hounds moved off for the covert. He quickened his pace then, and stole quietly down to a certain corner, which experience taught him was the likeliest place for a good start.

Burton Brake, a straggling covert of brush-wood and black-thorn, on the side of a hill, lay

immediately under a wide tract of downs. It
was a favourite resort of foxes; and, for some
unexplained reason, they usually went away
from it at the low side, to make a distant point
across the Vale. This was a flat, strongly-
fenced district, consisting chiefly of grass,
without a canal, or a river, or a railroad, or
even an impracticable brook. Its farm-houses
were few and far between; its enclosures large,
and wire was unknown. In good scenting
weather, it afforded almost the certainty of a
run, and, if he had a choice, a man did not
bring his *worst* horse to Burton Brake!

"He's away!" exclaïmed Miss Bruce, as
the quick notes of a horn came wafted up the
hill on the light easterly breeze.

"Who?" asked Nelly, shaking with excitement.

"The fox, my dear, of course. Look! I
can see the leading hounds. There, to the left
of the tall ash. Three or four specks of white
in that large green field. They're all coming
though, and the huntsman, and a black coat,

and four, five, six, red! Now they're at the
fence. Capital! One down, I'm afraid; and
he's let his horse go! Oh! I wish I was on
Safeguard! They're going to have the best
run that ever was seen!"

Fortunately for Nelly's peace of mind, the
fallen sportsman wore a dark coat, and,
therefore, could not be her husband. She
fancied, indeed, that she made him out amongst
the half-dozen riders who were nearest the
hounds.

Somehow it seemed less dangerous than she
had supposed, and infinitely better fun. Her
companions, too, were as eager for the sport as
if they had never been out hunting before.
Already they were consulting as to the best
line for a carriage to travel in the direction of
the chase.

"Into the Fosse again, Peter," said Lord
Fitzowen to the coachman. "Then to the
right and keep on the high ground. If they
turn to the downs, we shall command them
all the time."

"No, no, Lord Fitz," protested Hester. "He went away like a good fox, and with this wind he'll make his point for Brierley Bottoms. We had a nice gallop over the same line three weeks ago. There—I can see them bending to the left. Into Marigold Lane, Peter! down to Burton-Hayes, and if we don't come up with them at the Purlieus, make for Brierley Steeple as fast as you can!"

So Peter started his horses at so smart a trot as soon became a canter, using such dispatch, indeed, in Marigold Lane, notwithstanding its ruts and inequalities, as to overtake divers second-horsemen, a colt-breaker, a boy on a pony, and several more laggards of the chase.

"Do you think we shall ever see them again?" asked Nelly, straining her eyes to scan the extreme distance, eight or nine miles off. "I should like to know what becomes of the fox, only I hope they won't kill it, poor thing!"

"I hope they *will!*" replied Miss Bruce.

" Why, my dear Mrs. Roy, that's the one thing that makes a good run perfect. Look out! Lord Fitz. If they're coming to the Purlieus you ought to see something of them at the next turn."

" By Jove! There they are! Miss Bruce, you're a witch. No. You're a capital judge of hunting. They're checked, I do believe. They're all standing still in the lane. Bravo! They've hit it off again. Look! Mrs. Roy. Do you see the sheep running? That's the line of the fox. The hounds are right! He's crossed the brook. Now we shall have some fun!"

" It's practicable enough," said Hester. " I jumped it on Gondolier last season."

" They don't seem to think so! Hurrah! Three fellows are going to have it, four! five! Well done! There are two over, and one, I think, in for all day!"

Even at so long a distance Nelly's loving eyes had recognised her husband. He was safely landed on the right side, yet she turned pale to realise the risk he had run.

"One of those is Mr. Roy," she observed softly. "How beautifully he rides!"

"I didn't know he was out," commented Lord Fitzowen. "I never saw him at the Meet. You're quite right, Mrs. Roy, he *can* ride when he likes. He's going like a bird to-day!"

He *was* going well. A skilful horseman, experienced in the sport, riding a practised hunter that answered every turn of his hand, every pressure of his limbs, he found no difficulty in keeping close to the pack. Fence after fence, and field after field, were disposed of with the ease and confidence attained by a combination of good nerves, good riding, good condition, and good blood.

He went in and out of the lane not twenty yards from his wife, but so intent was he on the hounds, and the management of his horse, that he saw neither the carriage nor its occupants.

Nelly watched him with her heart in her eyes. The others, under pressure of that

mysterious law which compels everybody, out
hunting, to get somewhere else in a tremendous
hurry, were giving Peter many contrary
directions, that caused him, however, to put
his horses into a gallop, and make for a turn-
pike road with the utmost dispatch.

Over its harder surface, those who hunted
on wheels were able to hold their own with the
riders. They overtook, indeed, more than one
defeated sportsman, disappointed that his horse
could not gallop on for ever, or so far behind,
that he had pulled up in disgust; but, in
either case, plunged in the lowest depths of
misery, just as the first flight were raised to
the seventh heaven of enjoyment.

"There's Brierley Steeple!" exclaimed
Hester, pointing to the distant spire, with a
taper gloved hand. "It's down-hill all the
way to the village, and a capital road. I'll
never pilot anybody again, if we don't come
up with them now!"

But though Miss Bruce was right, and her
knowledge of fox-hunting did not mislead her

when she named Brierley Bottoms as the probable conclusion of the chase, it had come to a triumphant termination long before she could arrive at that rough and broken ravine. The fox had been eaten, the huntsman praised, the chosen few had exchanged enthusiastic compliments and congratulations. When the carriage stopped amongst them, they were already lighting their cigars, and preparing to go home.

CHAPTER XIII.

SWEET SYMPATHY.

AFTER a storm comes a calm; after keen excitement, a re-action, partly welcome for its repose, partly saddening for its depression. He who has been so fortunate as to go from end to end of a run with fox-hounds, to his own satisfaction, feels, strange to say, as if he had performed a good action. The past, which is perhaps capable of affording more definite pleasure than either the present or the future, seems truly delightful, till his blood cools down. Then he comes back into the world of reality, somewhat chilled and dispirited, as everybody, after childhood, must be, on first waking up from a dream.

John Roy caught sight of the carriage containing Nelly and her friends, as he put his horse into a trot on the firm surface of the high road—pleased to find, that after standing about for a quarter of an hour, the good animal, notwithstanding its exertions, was neither stiff nor lame. He was disposed to be praised, and, so to speak, patted on the back for his prowess, considering with reason that he had acquitted himself more than creditably in a manly exercise. It was as if cold water had been poured down his back to observe Lord Fitzowen, gesticulating on the front seat of the barouche, opposite his wife. He had not once thought of Fitz all the morning, nor, truth to tell, of Nelly, for more than fifty minutes. A wife's image is the last that occurs to a man while hounds are running hard—the juxtaposition of these two reminded him of them in the most unwelcome manner. He felt cross and put out—all the more that he was unable to explain why—and did not care if one of the offenders, or both, should be made aware of his ill-humour.

Hester, in a high state of excitement, was the first to accost him.

"What a good gallop, Mr. Roy! How I've been envying you! We went very well, considering we were in a carriage, and kept you in sight all the time!"

Of course the ruder he meant to be to his wife, the more politeness he showed Miss Bruce.

"You ought to have been on Safeguard or Gondolier," said he, with a most amiable smile. "It would have suited you exactly. Five-and-forty minutes, only one check, lots of jumping, and not above half-a-dozen fellows with the hounds."

Nelly tried in vain to catch his eye.

"We saw you," she exclaimed eagerly. "I was so frightened when you came to the river —the brook, I mean—Lord Fitzowen won't let me call it a river. How brave of you to leap it! I shut my eyes for fear you should be drowned, and when I opened them, there you were, safe over—the dear horse! I'm not afraid of horses. I should like to stroke his nose!"

Pained, disappointed, she looked imploringly

in her husband's face, while he left her unnoticed, to continue his conversation with Miss Bruce.

"We never touched the Purlieus. He was too hot to go in, and he left Burton Hayes half-a-mile to the right, so that it was almost straight, and grass every yard. From Burton Brake to Brierley can't be less than nine miles on the map—we must have come fully eight as the crow flies. It has been a real good thing. As far as I can make out, it's the same line you went three weeks ago, before the frost. No doubt it was the same fox, but he'll never show you a run, Miss Bruce, any more."

"I'm sorry they've killed it!" exclaimed Nelly, addressing herself to Lord Fitzowen, as nobody else seemed inclined to listen. "The poor fox! Think how happy he was this morning before we came. Curled up, fast asleep, among the bushes, like one's own dog on the hearth-rug. It *does* seem hard. Why must the pleasure of one creature be the pain of another? Why is there so much misery in the world?"

Such questions involved a train of deeper thought than Lord Fitzowen was in the habit of following out, and he answered vaguely—

"Yes, of course. It's a great pity, and all that. Still, you know, Mrs. Roy, when you go to find a fox, you must let the hounds hunt him, you know, and kill him if they can. It's wonderful how often they can't!"

She was trying to catch her husband's eye. What was there wrong? Why wouldn't he speak to her? She made one last despairing attempt.

"Mr. Roy," she said timidly, "couldn't—couldn't the servant take your horse, and you ride home in the carriage with us?"

He turned hot all over, feeling also that "he did well to be angry" now. These solecisms were intolerable! To offer him a seat in another lady's carriage was bad enough, but to propose he should *ride* in it! The woman would drive him mad!

Drawing his horse out of reach, for she was trying to pat its neck, he disposed of her ill-timed suggestion with the coldest of looks and in the unkindest of tones.

"I need not thank you for an invitation," said he, "that is not yours to give, and as I am rather wet, I prefer *riding* my horse to the *drive* you are good enough to offer me in a carriage that is not your own!" Then he took off his hat to Miss Bruce and disappeared.

Nelly was cut to the heart. Her eyes filled with tears. She had some difficulty in preventing their falling on her hands, and she was truly grateful to Lord Fitzowen when he diverted Hester's attention with an announcement that one of the horses was going lame. By the time the carriage could be stopped, and a pair of legs and feet carefully examined, to account for an infirmity that did not exist, Mrs. Roy had recovered her composure, and Fitz had earned an eternal claim to her gratitude and goodwill.

People are never so susceptible of kindness as when wounded by their nearest and dearest; nor is any gleam of sunshine so pale and watery, but that we welcome it on a wet day.

Nelly seemed sadly out of spirits during the rest of the drive. Miss Bruce, with a woman's quickness of perception, did not fail to detect something wrong. Lord Fitzowen accounted for feminine uneasiness of mind and body on a theory of his own. It originated, he believed, in a disorder peculiar to the sex, called "nerves," of which the seat, causes, and remedy were as yet undiscovered by science, and with which all the resources of medicine were powerless to contend.

But when they had dropped Nelly at her own door, declining the refreshment of tea, which she nearly omitted to offer, his anxiety prompted him to ask Hester whether she thought Mrs. Roy was as strong as she looked ? " People ought not to tire so easily, Miss Bruce ? " he observed gravely. " No lady can be well who is completely exhausted after a few hours' drive in an open carriage. Why, she hardly spoke a word all the way back ; and

did you observe how pale she was? Depend
upon it she's got nerves; nothing else punishes
them like that. It's a most distressing malady,
worse than measles, and they don't get over it
for weeks."

"Very likely," answered Hester. "You
seem to know all about it. I never had them
myself, and I hope I never shall. Now you
are to go on with the carriage, Lord Fitz, and
tell Papa I shall be home in half-an-hour. No,
I rather like the walk, and I'm not afraid of
crossing our own park by myself at any hour
of the day or night. Besides, I shall be back
long before dark."

"Mayn't I come with you?"

"Certainly not; you turn my dear old
ladies into ridicule, and I won't have it."

"But if I promise to be on my best
behaviour?"

"Your best behaviour is anybody else's
worst! I can't trust you directly my back is
turned. You're capable of making faces at
them, or any other enormity, if you're not

watched every moment. No, Lord Fitz, do as I bid you, and mind you tell Papa I shall not be late."

So Miss Bruce got out of the carriage, to the great delight of such villagers of Nether-Warden as chanced to be at their doors or in the street, and passing through a spacious walled garden, disappeared on the threshold of an old red-brick house, that professed to have been built in the reign of George II., and looked as if it had never been repaired nor altered since.

Lord Fitzowen proceeded homewards in the carriage ; but he, too, preferred to alight and walk the last half-mile of his journey, finding himself, for the first time in his life, so perplexed in mind as to feel disposed for solitary reflection.

This young nobleman's course had been hitherto shaped over smooth water and before a fair breeze. He had scarcely yet had any nut to crack harder than a letter to a lawyer, or felt any deeper interest than the lameness of

a horse. The world had been a pleasant place
enough; several people seemed to be put in it
on purpose to serve, and a few to amuse him.
There might be a certain sameness and want of
excitement about life, but if the roses offered
little fragrance, the thorns were by no means
sharp, and altogether it did very well. What
had come to him now, that thus had altered
the whole trim and bearings of his character,
opening his eyes, as it were, to the knowledge
of good and evil, scattering his Epicurean
philosophy to the winds? Things to which he
had attached a high value seemed all at once of
no importance, and illusions that he used to
consider the wildest and emptiest of dreams,
sprang into glowing life and reality, as at the
touch of a magic wand. "Is it my mind," he
thought, "that is affected, or—or is it my
heart? Let me light a cigar, and look at the
case fairly as it stands. Have I not everything
a man can reasonably require to make him
happy? Good health, good digestion, good
manners, without vanity, a good appearance,

and good horses, if they were only sound? What more can a fellow want, in such a position as mine, and amongst the people with whom I live? Is this strange sense of longing, half sweet, half bitter, and wholly inexplicable, only a craving for some new excitement, or is it an effort of the spirit, the soul, the *divinæ particula auræ*, the higher part of one's nature, to assert its individuality, and free itself from the material surroundings, with which we encumber it too much? It is not enough for the happiness of a thinking being to eat, drink, and smoke, ride a run, shoot a covert, play a cricket-match, and talk about it afterwards, from day to day, and year to year, till some fine morning the clock stops, the doctor can't wind it up, the umpire gives one 'out,' and so '*Bon soir, la compagnie!*' Why do I feel at this moment as if the finish would be less unwelcome, while yet life seems sweeter than usual? I know why, but I cannot bear to confess it even to myself. I never thought I should come to this! That I, of all people, should be haunted by tags

and ends of verses, should be able to understand
what a fellow means when he says—

> ' A livelier emerald twinkles in the grass,
> A softer sapphire melts upon the sea.'

I shall be writing poetry myself next. Already
I can make ' ass ' rhyme to ' grass,' and ' me '
to ' sea.'

" A sensible man would slip his cables, would
cut and run, while there was a chance of escape.
I am *not* a sensible man; I doubt very much
if I *want* to be saved from my own destruction.
I think I'd rather not. My visit comes to an
end to-morrow, but Sir Hector is sure to ask
me to stay another week. I *shall* stay another
week, I know, and I shall see Mrs. Roy again—
perhaps once, certainly not more than twice.
Never mind, once is better than nothing. It's
no use trying to deceive oneself. I love the
very ground that woman walks on—but in all
honour, and respect, and regard. I shall never
let her find it out, though women are very
quick to see things. At any rate, I shall never
tell her so. It would be an insult—an outrage.

But I am sure she is not happy. He does not half appreciate her. There *can* be no harm in my thinking of her, watching over her, serving her, and worshipping her in secret, as a true knight worshipped his mistress in the olden time!"

Arriving at this wise conclusion and the hall-door in the same moment, our modern Sir Galahad threw away his cigar, and stalked into the house, perfectly satisfied with his own special pleading, and the integrity of his relations towards Mrs. Roy.

CHAPTER XIV

Two gaunt women, so like each other that Lord Fitzowen christened them Gog and Magog, rose simultaneously when Hester entered the room. It was pleasant to see the smile of affection that brightened those grim faces while they kissed her forehead, and offered their own brown, leathery cheeks to be saluted in return.

The Miss Brails, or rather the Misses Brail, as they preferred to be called, were two spinsters, long resident in Nether-Warden, of whom Miss Bruce had made an easy conquest from the first week she came to live at the Towers. Unlike most old ladies, they owned no pets, never having possessed anything of the kind indeed but a bullfinch that moulted

and died ten days after purchase. Their new
neighbour, therefore, seemed to infuse an
element of affection, mirth, and gladness into
their lives, of which, having little experience,
they valued the novelty no less than the
intrinsic delight. Said Gog to Magog, "We
couldn't love that dear girl better if she was a
daughter of our own." Answered Magog,
unequal to realise the supposed relationship,
"Not half so well, my dear. Hester seems like
a daughter and a niece and a sister all in one."

Miss Bruce returned their attachment with
a warmth and cordiality that puzzled even
Sir Hector, who knew his child's character
better than anybody.

"I don't wonder at the old ladies," said he
to Lord Fitzowen one day after dinner.
"That's not surprising. Everybody likes
Hester. One might as well say one didn't
like this '64 claret ; but what she can see in
them, that beats me, I own. And I used to
think I understood women as well as most
people."

A great many men think the same : always
the more persistently the less they know of the
gentler and subtler sex.

Perhaps only Hester could have told him
why she loved Gog and Magog so dearly. It
is my opinion, however, that she admitted her
reasons even to herself with great reservation,
and would have died a hundred deaths rather
than confide them to another.

"No. I've not come to tea," explained the
visitor, as one hostess felt for her keys, and the
other bustled into the passage with the words
"Hot buttered toast" on her lips. "It's hours
too early. Besides, I must go back and make
his for Papa. I can't stay a moment. I only
rushed in, on my way home, to see that you
were both alive. I haven't been here for two
whole days."

"Take off your hat and warm your feet,"
said Gog, while Magog wheeled an arm-chair
to the hearth-rug. "It does our very hearts
good to see you," continued both spinsters
in a breath. "Don't stay a moment more

than you ought, but as long as ever you can."

After they had settled her comfortably before the fire, there was a pause in the conversation, borne somewhat impatiently by the young lady, who broke it at last with the single monosyllable,—

"Well?"

Gog and Magog looked in each other's faces, and began simultaneously, "Good news, my dear. The best of news. You tell her, sister,— No. I will. Dear, dear, it seems like a dream."

"Not both at once," protested Hester, trying bravely to smile, though her face was very pale, and her heart beat fast.

"We've seen a letter," said Gog.

"A *ship*-letter, my dear," interrupted Magog.

"A letter is a letter," observed Miss Bruce, "whether it comes by land or sea. Is the expedition on its way home, and—and— Are they all safe?"

She was a brave girl; but, do what she

would, her voice trembled, and her very lips turned white.

"We have scarcely thought about *all* of them," answered Magog, blowing her nose because tears were in her eyes. "It's enough for us that Coll. has been preserved."

"We are selfish creatures," added Gog. "But we have only one nephew left on earth, and he can't be the same thing to other people that he is to us."

Miss Bruce seemed to doubt the position, but this was no time to dispute it, and she could only exclaim, "Then he has got back alive. Thank God!"

"Thank God!" repeated the spinsters reverently, and all three women kept silence for the space of nearly thirty seconds!

"When—when is he coming to see you?" faltered Hester, whose feminine imagination had already overleapt weeks and months, leagues of blue water, duty on board ship, Admiralty leave, and all other practical obstacles at a bound.

"Oh! my dear, we mustn't think of such a treat yet," answered Magog. "He writes from Spitzbergen—you know, that's some place in the arctic regions, but it's nothing to do with the North Pole. You understand, my sister found it on the map, and it looks a long way off even there. But it is always a stage on the homeward journey; and as I told her this morning, it does not seem so presumptuous to hope we shall see him back now."

"In a month or six weeks at farthest," said Gog, whose late geographical researches gave her opinion considerable weight. "They have put in to refit, as he calls it, for it seems they couldn't get good butcher's meat nor vegetables, nor anything wholesome to eat up there. I fancy it's a wild, dismal kind of place; but Coll. never complains, put him where you will, never did from a boy. There's his letter, my dear young lady. You can read it for yourself. Doesn't he write a fine, clear, bold hand for a sailor? I began to teach him before he could speak plain. What a to-do he

made with his pen! His mother said she
never saw so many blots on one page in her
life before. Ah! she was glad enough to get
that dirty piece of paper you have in your
hand: but I dare say she never thought who
set him his first copy, and in my opinion she
ought to have sent it on to my sister and me
without losing a post!"

Hester did not answer. She was far away
among floes and icebergs and eternal snow,
with the writer of those flimsy, close-written
pages, that had reached her from regions which
to us who sit at home at ease are as another
world. The very paper seemed redolent of tar,
tobacco, salt water, perilous adventure, and the
discipline of a man-of-war, as she held it near
her face, partly to conceal her agitation, partly
to decipher the clear, fine characters, faded
somewhat in their transmission through so
many climates, over so wide an expanse of sea.
She made it all out, nevertheless, though her
own brimming eyes failed her more than once
ere she came to an end of the following sketch

from a sailor's life in search of the North
Pole :—

"H.M.S. Aurora, off Spitzbergen.

"Dearest Mother,—I wrote you at some
length nearly a year ago. You will be expecting another letter soon, but when you get this,
the Expedition will be well on its way home.
I shall hope to see you and all my kind friends
in old England once again before next spring.
We shall come back with flying colours. If we
have failed in our great object (and between
you and me, I don't think the plank will ever
be sawn that shall float our flag under the
North Pole), still we have made many important
discoveries, and smoothed the way for all who
wish to follow in our wake, and fetch the
extreme point at which we were turned back.
If they can make more northing, let 'em! I
for one will give them three cheers.

"Our skipper has proved himself a trump.
I always told you he would, and I should be
afraid to say whether officers or men have done

their duty most thoroughly and ungrudgingly.
I never heard a wry word nor a complaint, and
that is something to say, mother, when you are
boxed up with your mates, and nothing but
your mates, for eleven months at a spell. Jolly
cold, too, I can tell you, more than half your
time. Our ship's surgeon is as good a chap as
ever broke a biscuit. I showed him to you at
Portsmouth when you came on board the
Scorpion, and I remember you thought him
very young. He looks older now, and so do I ;
but ours has been a roughish job, and if he
hadn't been wiser than he looked, some of us
must have been disrated that time when the
lime-juice gave out. We've had no sickness
since, and, thank God, we hope to land the
whole ship's company, man for man, with a
clean bill of health, able and willing as when
they came on board. But it was close shaving
with some of us, now and again ; for it's not
easy, you know, in these high latitudes to
make fair weather of it all your time. A
pleasure-trip is one thing, and a voyage of

discovery another. I had rather a squeak for it myself, and I thought my mate—as fine a young fellow as ever stepped—must have left his bones, for he had very little else to leave, many a league within the Arctic Circle. It's a long story, what we call a *yarn* at sea, but you would like to know, and I will tell you all about it.

" After we had taken up a warm berth, and made the ship snug for the winter amongst the ice, we were told off in exploring parties, well found in dogs, sledges, and rations to cruise about here, there, and everywhere, by compass, you understand, but always creeping, inch by inch, towards the north. When it came to my turn of duty I had the command of one of these—six in number, all told—three fore-top-men, a gunner's mate, the ship's carpenter, and myself. I need not tell you how many days we were absent, nor how little way we made in proportion to the labour and the hardship, and at last the bodily suffering we had to undergo. Our blue-jackets don't sing out

before they're hurt, nor yet for some little
time after, I fancy; and mine were as smart a
lot of men as you could pick from the whole
ship's company.   But flesh and blood can't
make it out in such stress of weather as we had
to face, when the stores get lów, and at last we
were forced to separate.   I sent three of the
men back to the ship, carrying with them the
fourth, who was disabled, on the only sledge
left.   The other had been burnt for firewood,
and the dogs—don't turn sick, mother—killed
and eaten, long ago.   I pushed on one more
day's march with the carpenter, however, to
take the bearings of a long, low spit of land
that wasn't down in any of our charts, and I
thought, God forgive me ! what a fine thing it
would be for this unknown promontory to be
called ever after by my own name, Cape
Collingwood, we'll say, or, perhaps, Cape Brail !
Well, if this was vanity I took my punishment
for it smart and soon.   We never made it out
after all.   There were great fissures in the ice
to be weathered, and for every cable's length

ahead we were bound to walk, or, I shall say
to roll and tumble, like a brace of black fish,
for a league.· The third day it came on to blow
a whirlwind,—of snow, mind you. We lost
our bearings, we lost our own backward track,
we knew that of our mates must have been
covered long ago. There was nothing for it
but to steer by compass, in hope of making the
ship before our strength gave out completely
from fatigue and starvation.

"Till I overhauled the ship's log afterwards,
I could not have told you how many days we
were out, drifting over the ice, without a
morsel of food. We lost count of them, for as
we got weaker in our bodies we turned queer
in our heads. Giddy and snow-blind, one of
us would fall now and again, unable to see
where he set his feet, and it was a job for his
mate to put him back on his pins. Had both
been down at once, we should never have got
up any more.

"At last the carpenter turned silly altogether. He plodded on soberly enough, but

wandered in his talk, jawing incessantly of the
garden at home, and the bee-hives. What
should make a man think of bee-hives at the
North Pole?—and running water—he heard it
behind him, he declared, and must go back to
see for himself. Then I had to pinion his arms
and force him to keep with me. It wasn't
much of a struggle, we were as weak as two cats ;
still we kept walking on, like men in a dream.

"It seemed lonely enough, but we didn't
ask for company ; at least, not for the company
that dropped in on us when we were at our
lowest and worst. I've heard of a man being
followed step for step by a ghost. I don't
know how he liked it, but I think no ghost
could have followed quieter, softer, with a more
stealthy even noiseless foot than the creature
that was waiting on us, sometimes forty, sometimes twenty, sometimes not more than ten
paces in our wake. There is no animal so
patient, so wary, so sagacious, and so persevering as the white arctic bear, when he has
made up his mind for a meal.

" I couldn't hear him, he stepped so smooth and silent, pace for pace, with ourselves ; but somehow, before I turned and saw him, I *felt* he was there !

" The brute knew well enough we must soon sink from fatigue. He could finish us off then without risk or trouble, so was quite content to wait, and eat us up at his leisure.

" I don't think the carpenter knew anything about this ugly consort. He kept rambling on with his bee-hives and his running water. When he spoke loud, the bear would fall back a little ; when his voice sank, it came on with longer strides. At last I fancied I could hear its breathing, and the fall of its flat, soft paws on the snow.

" My mate stumbled and came down. We were both so weak that with all my exertions I could not get him up again. Faint and breathless I rested for a minute by his side. The bear reared itself on end, as if to see what it could make of us, and, finding both motionless, came on steadier than before.

"I had a single-barrelled gun, loaded with slugs. I kept them for the chance of a seal. It would have been sheer madness to use such a charge except at close quarters, and I lay quiet like a dead man behind my mate's body, with my finger on the trigger.

"How I cursed the creature's cunning, and the time it kept me in suspense, while it stopped and snuffed and walked in circles round us, as if it had some suspicion of the trick. My mate was very drowsy, and I knew well that if once he went to sleep it would all be over. Forty winks in such a cold as that means never unbuttoning your eye-lids again!

"But the beast was hungry—famished. I could see threads of slaver waving over its breast and paws. After a minute or two it could resist no longer, and stole softly on to us, stirring the carpenter with its nose, as if to make sure he was really dead.

"Then I pulled. The muzzle of my gun was close under its shoulder, and the charge passed through its heart like a bullet. I jumped

up among the smoke, and used all the strength
I had left to haul my mate out of reach, lest it
should strike him in the death-flurry; but the
creature made a decent end enough, going off
quiet and easy, like a Christian.

" 'Turn and turn about,' says I, 'you
meant to eat *us;* but I think we shall more
likely eat you!' Don't call me a cannibal,
mother; I was forced to drink some of the
blood warm, to put strength in me, before I
could turn to and recover my mate. He was
nearly gone. Five minutes more would have
done his business; but he came to, and he
pulled through, even at this moment I could
hardly tell you how or why.

" We camped out by the carcase, and fed
on it till our strength came back. I don't
know how long. We had been seventeen days
out, when we returned to the ship. I was
proud of what the skipper said to me, and
the men gave us three cheers as we came up
the side.

" This is a long story, mother, but I've

plenty like it in store for you when we meet.
I will say no more now, for I have come to the
end of my paper, and it won't be many weeks
before you will welcome back, like a bad shilling,
your affectionate son, Collingwood Brail.

"P.S. Please send this on, for my good
aunts to read. If it saves trouble, they need
not mind showing it to anybody they please."

She would have liked to go over it all again,
particularly the postscript, which, some strange
intuition taught her, contained an exceedingly
roundabout message for herself; but a woman's
first impulse in such cases is to conceal the
truth, and she returned the precious sheets
with the utmost calmness she could assume.

"I was sure you would be pleased to hear,"
said Magog, pocketing the document. "You
have always interested yourself in him for our
sake, and, indeed, if you knew Coll. better, I
believe you would like him for his own."

Many things might be less improbable, for
which reason, perhaps, Miss Bruce did not

think it worth while to pursue the subject, but bade the old ladies a hasty farewell, kissing each of them with even greater cordiality than before.

As Gog observed to her sister, when the door closed on their charming visitor, "That girl grows handsomer every day. Did you see what a beautiful colour she had just now, as she went out?"

"It's unwholesome for people to sit over the fire," answered practical Magog; "I only hope she may not take cold on her way home."

Sir Hector, too, thought his daughter seemed in unusual spirits when she gave him his tea. The day's doings, the drive out, the drive back, above all the run from Burton Brake, were detailed with more than her customary gaiety and playfulness. Lord Fitz-owen, sitting alone with his host after dinner, found his own account completely forestalled. Even the abruptness with which Mr. Roy "snubbed his poor wife" seemed to have been duly reported, and if Fitz grew somewhat prolix over this unpleasant episode, it was more for his own satisfaction than the information of his friend.

Before they adjourned to the drawing-room, however, Sir Hector changed the conversation by warmly pressing his guest to defer the departure fixed for next day, and remain at least a week longer at Warden Towers, an invitation Lord Fitzowen accepted gratefully. "It would be rude to decline," he thought, "when they make such a point of it, and, after all, I should be just as great a fool about her anywhere else as here!"

CHAPTER XV.

THE LITTLE RIFT.

JOHN ROY, like most men who can command a choice of apartments, had selected the most uncomfortable room in the house for his own. Here he smoked, sulked, wrote his letters, and brooded over his wife's " want of manner " in complete privacy, for even Nelly had been made to understand that, unless by special invitation, her presence was unwelcome in this retreat. It saddened her to reflect for how many hours in the day her husband preferred to be alone. She was beginning to wonder whether he had done wisely in marrying her; to feel, with much bitter heart-searching and humiliation, that she was a clog round his neck; and, indeed, though he ought to have been ashamed to confess it, John Roy told himself the same story over and over again. He compared her with the women he used to meet in London society during his early life, and was so bad a judge as to rate her their inferior because her nature was different from theirs. Yet he would have felt indignant to be told he was the sort of man who could prefer a camelia to a garden-rose.

Though one tried hard to conceal it from herself, and the other from the world, both were conscious of a breach between them that widened day by day, rendering the husband irritable, captious, and aggressive, the wife nervous, silent, and depressed.

He could not but observe her fading colour and weary, heavy eyes, that seemed afraid to meet his own. When people came to call, she would brighten up; which provoked him exceedingly, although this improvement in her spirits was partly the result of a wish to please him by taking her share in general conversation, partly the natural protest of youth and health against despondency. With none of her visitors

did she seem so much at ease as with Lord
Fitzowen, and Mr. Roy had already asked
himself why, more than once. "Hang him!
he's never out of the house!" was the form
into which he put his reflections, seeing that
ere the run from Burton Brake was a week old
his lordship had already called twice.

So John Roy sat after breakfast in his own
den, revolving these unpleasant thoughts behind
the *Field* or "Country Gentleman's Newspaper,"
making believe to read its innumerable columns
with their miscellaneous contents. "Come in!"
he exclaimed impatiently, as a hesitating knock
announced an interruption. He thought it
was Nelly, and felt so vexed with her that he
determined to let her see that he would rather
be alone.

It was *not* his wife, but Mrs. Mopus, who
shut the door carefully, set her back to it, and
stood there, pale, panting, with one hand
pressed against her side.

He was prepared to be angry, yet he showed
no irritation towards his housekeeper as he laid

down the newspaper and asked quietly " What he could do for her?"

"Can I speak a word with you, sir?" said Mrs. Mopus, advancing to the middle of the room and looking about, as if for a soft place to faint away. "I'm sure I beg your pardon, sir. You'll forgive me, Mr. Roy. It's not of my own free will I come here to-day."

"Then why are you standing there?" was the natural rejoinder, but certain catchings of the breath, which his experience of women had taught him to mistrust, prevented its utterance, and he was content to observe, courteously—

"Compose yourself, Mrs. Mopus; you have generally a good reason for everything you do."

To beg of a lady that she will "compose herself" seldom produces the desired effect until after many repetitions and much soothing, by implication, no less than in set terms. Mrs. Mopus thought well to gasp, roll her eyes, and wrap both hands in her black silk apron, till a shower of tears came to her relief, and she found voice to explain between the sobs—

"Oh! sir, you won't judge hardly of me for my attachment to you and yours. Indeed, Mr. Roy, when I think of harm that's likely to overtake you, I'm that upset I can hardly look in your face and warn of you in time, if indeed it's not too late already; but they do say fore-warned is fore-armed, and though you was to turn me out of doors this moment, without a character or a month's notice, you should never be left in ignorance by *me*. No, not if I was to die for it the next minute. There!"

"I have assured you very often, Mopus, that I am convinced of your regard," he answered kindly. "But if you and I are to understand each other, I must beg you to speak out and tell me what is the matter."

"Mr. Roy, do you never think of the times when you was unmarried? A free, well-spoken, handsome young gentleman as any lady might be happy to call her own, if she was the highest in the land?"

"Well, what of that? I made my choice

and married once for all—good or bad, it's too
late to repent now."

"Good or bad, sir. You never said a truer
word. When I think of them as would have
been proud to take your name, and her as has
it this day, but doesn't seem to value it not one
halfpenny, it makes me that mad—that—well
—that it sets me on to come into this room,
though I *am* only a servant, and speak with
you, fair and equal, Mr. Roy, like a friend."

"You *are* a friend, Mopus. I am ready to
hear all you have to communicate."

"Mr. Roy, you'll excuse me, the lady that
you have made my mistress and your wife
didn't ought to be neither the one nor the
other."

"Take care what you say, Mrs. Mopus.
Is this only an expression of opinion, or is it an
accusation to which you can bring proof?"

His voice shook, and he was fain to turn
his head, that she might not see how his
countenance changed. A hundred conflicting
feelings were at work in his heart. Could this

woman show him a way to the freedom he had
of late desired too earnestly? and if so, would
he consent to pay the price? To give up
Nelly did not seem so difficult, but that she
should cease to care for him was another matter
altogether. The bare suspicion struck him with
a sense of keen and numbing pain. Release
might be bought too dear. What if the blow
were so roughly dealt that in striking away the
fetter it should break the bone!

Mrs. Mopus eyed him narrowly. She had
studied his temper all those years to little
purpose if she could not play on it now, like
an instrument of music, to wake whatever chord
she pleased.

"Mr. Roy," she said, coming a step nearer,
"I wish to give up my situation."

"Why, Mrs. Mopus?" he asked, with some
discomposure, surprised, no doubt, by the
unexpected nature of her attack.

"Because, sir, it is not my place as a servant
to speak so free as I could wish. When you
have discharged me, Mr. Roy, I cease to be a

servant, and my words will come easier, as I said before, from the lips of a humble friend."

"Nonsense! I am not going to lose you for any such foolish fancies. You don't want to leave, my good woman, and I don't want to part with you; I am tired of assuring you that I feel you have my interest at heart. If you know anything that affects my welfare, it is your duty to inform me frankly and without reserve."

"You'll promise not to be angry with *me*, sir. I wouldn't offend you for more than I can say."

"I promise."

"And you'll never disclose who it was as told you, nor mention my name, nor let anybody know that you and me has been talking secrets together on such a matter as this?"

He nodded impatiently.

Mrs. Mopus seemed well accustomed to plotting. She peered cautiously into the passage to make sure nobody was listening, shut the door softly, and came close to her master's chair.

"It's about your lady, sir," she whispered. "Have I your good leave, Mr. Roy, to speak my mind?"

"Go on!"

"She's not a lady as ought to be at the head of your house, sir. I pass over her inter-ference with the upper servants and the tradespeople, her pryings about in the kitchen, the scullery, the offices, even to the soft-water pump in the back yard. I am willing to believe it's the faults of her bringing-up; that's neither here nor there. But she doesn't respect *you*, Mr. Roy; she doesn't think as much of you as she ought. She has a free way with the gentlemen, that isn't becoming in *your* lady, and with one in particular, I don't name no names, but I've seen it from the time he came here first. I've kept it down, Mr. Roy, till I thought I should have suffocated, but now you've asked me, sir, and it's come out at last plump and plain!"

Vexation, perhaps, would express the nature of her listener's feelings better than surprise; yet with the common impulse of humanity to be convinced of its own worst suspicions, he came to the point at once and spoke out peremptorily enough.

"Let us understand each other, Mrs. Mopus. You have said too much or too little. You have observed freedom of conduct on the part of my—of Mrs. Roy, in respect to a certain person. I insist on knowing who this person is."

"Well, sir, if I must speak out, it's that there Lord. He's in the house now."

John Roy glanced at the clock on his chimney-piece. Half-past eleven. This was a morning visit with a vengeance! If the woman spoke truth in the present instance she was probably right all through.

"You are sure of what you say?" he asked, rising from his chair with some vague idea of immediate action.

"Satisfy yourself, Mr. Roy," was the answer. "They're in the conservatory feeding

the gold fish at this moment. I see them
through the back-staircase window as I come
down to you."

He was so angry he could hardly trust
himself to speak.

"Enough, Mrs. Mopus," he muttered, "I
shall not forget your services;" and regardless
of her entreaties that he would calm himself,
would do nothing rash, he hurried out of the
room and up the back-staircase aforesaid to
confront the culprits in the conservatory, and—
and—What further steps was he to take when
he got there?

This consideration caused him to pause ere
he had threaded two dark passages on the way
to his destination. He could neither kick, nor
shoot, nor turn a gentleman out of the house
for paying his wife a visit after breakfast rather
than after luncheon, nor would any social code
hold him justified in making two persons
responsible for a serious offence because they
gave his gold fish their dinners before twelve
o'clock in the day!

He stopped—he hesitated—he went on
again, still towards the conservatory, but much
slower than before.   It would be rather tame,
he thought, to walk in with outstretched hand,
and say, "How d'ye do, Fitzowen.   Won't you
stay to luncheon?" but there seemed nothing
else for it, so irresistible are our bonds of
custom, our usages of society.   The verdict of
the world is dead against a man who "puts
himself in the wrong," and it is amusing to
watch how, even as two practical fighters shift
and traverse to get their backs to the sun, so
in a personal difference, or an angry corre-
spondence, the belligerents by dint of argument,
reply, and rejoinder, find at last the position
completely inverted, and each occupying his
adversary's ground.

"I had better seem to suspect nothing,"
said John Roy to himself.   "I must watch
them, and draw my own conclusions unobserved."

His hand was on the conservatory door, he
had no intention of eavesdropping; nothing

would have induced him so far to lower himself
in his own esteem; but he paused an instant
to compose his features and pull himself
together, as it were, for the ordeal. In that
instant his wife's low sweet voice, deepened
and softened by emotion, struck on his ear.

"I am horribly afraid of offending Mr.
Roy," she said; "but I can trust you un-
reservedly, and will always do whatever you
think best!"

CHAPTER XVI.

THE MUSIC MUTE.

IT was the old story. Neither in conversation nor in literature can you rightly interpret a sentence without the context. Mrs. Roy's compromising words did but conclude a conference of which, as far as she was concerned, loyalty to her husband had been the one predominant motive.

Sir Hector was confined to his room by gout, the other guests had departed; it was impossible for Lord Fitzowen to remain at Warden Towers alone with Miss Bruce, and, sorely against his inclinations, he felt that in common decency he must return to London by the afternoon train. All this he explained at great length, while excusing himself for paying Mrs. Roy so early a visit to wish her good-bye.

Perhaps he cherished some vague hope of an invitation to Royston Grange. If so, it was speedily dispelled; for though Nelly assured him frankly enough that she was sorry he must go away, she added in the same breath, " We shall all be better for a little rest. I am a very quiet person, Lord Fitzowen, and we've had so much dining out lately and so many visitors, it will seem quite a relief to be alone."

This was a damper, and he felt it. She spoke as if she would be glad to get rid of him. Fitz rather lost his head, and became so earnest that she took the alarm.

" I shall be wretched to go, Mrs. Roy. I never was so happy in my life as for this last fortnight, and I have *you* to thank for it." His voice trembled with that suppressed feeling which no woman is too inexperienced to understand.

" You have already thanked me by coming to say good-bye," she answered rather stiffly. " Besides, I don't like to be thanked, Lord

Fitzowen, when I have done nothing to deserve it."

She meant him to "keep his distance," and spoke more gravely than usual, but the warmest expressions of good-will would not have been calculated to rivet his fetters so securely. It is in these ups and downs, these sudden changes, that men become malleable, as the glowing iron is plunged in cold water that it may be tempered into steel.

He skipped back to safe ground with praiseworthy agility. "I like this country so much," he said, "and the hunting and my host and hostess. Don't you think Miss Bruce a very nice girl, Mrs. Roy?"

"I do indeed," she answered, wondering how she could have been so stupid as to forget that, of course, this was the cause of Lord Fitzowen's unwillingness to depart, and resolved to make him amends for her previous misconception. "I like her exceedingly. Not so well as *you* do, I dare say, but very much indeed. She must be sorry to lose you, though

I suppose we shall have you back before long."

He stared. Did she want him back? It was but a moment since she had seemed glad he must go away. He would have given a good deal to read her thoughts, and after all she was only hoping he wouldn't stay to luncheon, and wondering whether she ought to ask him or not!

"One hates saying good-bye," he continued, "and yet there is a melancholy satisfaction in it, too. Let us go and look at the gold fish, Mrs. Roy. I should not be easy if I went away without taking leave of my earliest friends."

So they strolled into the conservatory, where his lordship, who was not usually so diffident, debated in his own mind whether he dared ask her to give him a sprig of geranium. Had he done so, she would have complied with a readiness that showed how little importance she attached to the gift, but his courage failed him, and he preferred not to run the chance of a refusal, perhaps of another rebuff.

He was sinking deeper and deeper at every step. Had Fitz been wise, he would never have risked this last interview, but would have started for London with his valet and portmanteaus by the twelve o'clock train.

He looked at the gold fish in silence, almost wishing he was one of them that he might not be going away, then turned to Mrs Roy and said, with something of a sigh—

"You will miss your dictionary a little, won't you, when it is out of reach on the shelf?"

"I shall indeed," she answered kindly. " I am bad at thanking people, Lord Fitzowen, but I am not ungrateful. I shall never forget how friendly and considerate you have been with me. Though I don't say much, I feel things, I can tell you."

"Whenever you are in any way at a loss, Mrs. Roy, you have only got to speak the word. I would come from the other end of the world to be of the slightest use. You may want advice now and then about those absurd trifles in which my whole life has been spent."

"I feel dreadfully ignorant sometimes, Lord Fitzowen, I confess. I don't mind for myself, but it vexes my husband. He seems so annoyed with things that I should not have thought of the slightest importance."

He took her hand. "Then we will make a bargain," said he. "You shall be the conjurer and I'll be the Jack-in-the-box. Touch a spring and up he comes! When you've done with him, shut down the lid. Seriously, make any use of me you please when you don't want to trouble our friend. I dare say he hates being bothered. Most men do. I like it. Suppose you are in a dilemma, a social difficulty of any kind, consult me as if I was your cousin, or your brother, or your solicitor. I don't manage my own matters well, but I can give other people better advice than anybody in the world."

There was no resisting the hearty off-hand manner, the frank genial tone. Nelly thought she had discovered a wise counsellor, a true friend, and accepted his somewhat vague offer with the grateful little speech that so offended her husband's ears as he came in.

There was an awkward silence. Mrs. Roy looked and felt in a false position, though she could not have explained why. The master of the house seemed by no means master of the situation. Even his lordship, though more used to the kind of thing, was obviously ill-at-ease. He took the initiative, however, by putting out his hand and informing his host he had ridden over to say "Good-bye."

"Among the flowers," answered John Roy, looking round him with something of sarcasm, while he exchanged a farewell with his visitor readily enough. It was no prolonged ceremony, and before Nelly's flushed cheeks had faded to their usual tint, Lord Fitzowen vanished, leaving husband and wife alone with the gold fish.

These could not be more mute than John Roy. He shrugged his shoulders, put on that expression of contempt she most dreaded, and would have retired without a word, but that Nelly's heart was full to overflowing, and the appeal rose spontaneously to her lips—

"What have I done to deserve this? Why are you so cross with me, Mr. Roy?"

"Ask yourself."

"No. I ask *you*. We have not been married a year—nothing like it—and already you are tired of me, and you wish I was dead. You do—you do—and so do I. Anything would be better than this. You hate me, you avoid me. I never see you from day's end to day's end, and when we *are* alone together— which we *never* are—you won't speak to me. I am a clog, an encumbrance, a wet blanket! I can't imagine what it is I have done, or not done. Where are mine accusers? You ought to tell me. I've a right to know."

"When you can talk sense," he answered, "perhaps we may come to some understanding. I confess it seems hopeless now."

"You used to think different. You told

me at Beachmouth I was the most sensible woman you ever met."

"That was not saying much. I never had a high opinion of your sex. It does not improve on acquaintance."

"If you think that, it's cruel to tell me. If you don't think it, you oughtn't to say so. You can be all smiles and good-humour with other ladies. You don't call *them* a pack of fools to their faces. I used to believe you cared for me, or else why did you make me an offer? It would have been a long time before I asked *you;* and now you seem to like other people so much better than me!"

"Two can play at that game."

"What do you mean?" she flashed out. "Mr. Roy, I require you to explain yourself."

He set his lips tight, and spoke in cold, cutting syllables.

"Then I *will* explain myself. When a lady receives one of her husband's friends day after day, and at all hours, as you receive Lord Fitzowen, it is rather too good a joke that she should reproach that husband with want of attention to herself."

The tears came to her eyes; he must care for her a little, she reflected, or it would not matter to him how often Lord Fitz chose to call, or how long he stayed, but womanly pride and what is called "proper feeling" prompted her to affect a deeper indignation than she felt.

"Mr. Roy," she said, looking him full in the face, "do you assert what you know, or are you making these accusations against me to put yourself in the right?"

"I make no accusations," he replied, in the same hard tone. "It's not worth while. I simply use my own faculties like other people. Things are not likely to escape my observation that have become the talk of my servants in the kitchen and the hall."

She turned pale to her lips. "The servants!" she repeated. "Do you mean to tell me, Mr. Roy, that you have been discussing with your servants the conduct of your wife?"

He was getting very angry, he felt so completely in the wrong; therefore he affected to take high ground.

"I decline to enter into that subject," said he, "though *you* may choose to disregard both, there *are* people who respect my character and value my happiness. It is all very well, Mrs. Roy, to carry things with a high hand, to affect injured innocence, virtuous indignation, and so forth, but nobody shall make me believe that lady's conduct is irreproachable on whom her very domestics cry shame. Even if I had not eyes and ears of my own, I can trust my informant, and what I say I mean!"

Her sweet and gentle temper was roused at last. She moved to the door.

"Then if that is the position I occupy in your house," she exclaimed, "the sooner I leave it the better!"

"I wish you had never come into it!"

The action was over. Completely disabled by this last shot, poor Nelly struck her flag, and went down. She made no attempt at reply. She did not burst into tears, nor go off in hysterics, nor faint dead away, which is the best resource of all, as placing the adversary in such a position that he can neither run nor fight. She only paced slowly out of the conservatory, across the hall, and up the staircase to her own room, faltering and stumbling, though it was broad daylight, like a blind woman, or one who walks in a dream.

John Roy turned to the gold fish, and made them a little speech. "I have given her a piece of my mind at last," said he, somewhat ashamed of himself, yet with a certain amount of relief at having blown off the steam. "A man should begin as he means to go on, and she will be none the worse for the lesson. That it may take proper effect, I shall *not* see her again till dinner-time. My horse is at the door. I may as well have luncheon with the Grantons, and ride round by Warden Towers afterwards, to find out if this young lord is really gone."

Nelly, kneeling by her bedside, crying

bitterly with her face smothered in the counterpane, heard his horse's hoofs crunching the gravel, and the click of the gate as he turned into the park.

She went to her window and watched him, hiding behind the curtain. She had often seen him ride away in the same direction, but never so indistinctly as now, through a mist of tears.

Then she bathed her eyes, smoothed her hair, looked at a time-table, rang the bell, and ordered the carriage to be at the door in twenty minutes.

"If I had a baby," thought Nelly; "I couldn't go. I should neither have the heart to leave it, nor to take it away from Mr. Roy. How lucky for *him*. He will be happy at last. He won't miss me one bit. He can live among the people he likes without a wife that he is ashamed of at every turn. And yet I *did* try hard to be all he wished! Oh! my darling, my darling! I do believe my heart is breaking, but I will never see you again!"

Mr. Roy did not enjoy his luncheon. The

Grantons were pleasant as usual. Her two
pretty sisters, lately imported by the hostess,
did the agreeable with the vivacity shown by
young ladies at that most cheerful of meals.
But, somehow, it was all flat and insipid.
When his horse was brought round, he departed
in worse spirits than he arrived, conscious he
had made no favourable impression on the
strangers, but utterly careless of their opinion,
good or bad.

"Talking him over" ere he was fairly in
the saddle, these did not scruple to express
unqualified disappointment. Mr. Roy was
older, greyer, stupider, than they had been led
to expect, yet each told herself there was
something interesting about the man, something
strange, mysterious, peculiar, that she would
like to fathom and find out.

At Warden Towers, Sir Hector was in his
room, and Miss Bruce in the village, so he did
not get off. "Was Lord Fitzowen still with
them?" he asked carelessly, turning to go away.

"No; his lordship left after luncheon.

His lordship's letters were to be forwarded to London. He (the butler) did not think his lordship would be back again during the hunting season."

Riding home in the fading twilight, John Roy began to wonder if he had not judged Nelly too hastily in one particular, perhaps too harshly in all. There is something in the action of a good horse under a man, especially at a gallop, that, possibly through its effect on the liver, seems to clear and stimulate his brain. Ere he rode into his own stable-yard, our friend had resolved to be forgiving and magnanimous, to read his wife a long lecture on that ignorance of conventionalities to which he was willing to attribute her late misdeeds, and graciously to overlook the past in consideration of the amendment she was sure to promise for the future. Then he would proceed comfortably to dinner, and slumber placidly afterwards, having dismissed the whole subject from his mind.

Wet and muddy, he went to dress at once,

rehearsing during his toilet the discourse he
intended to deliver, and descending in half an
hour or so to the drawing-room, where he
expected to find his wife at her needlework,
bright with her usual welcome, and ready to
offer the cup of tea she had kept hot in case it
should be wanted. But here were neither wife
nor tea. The fire had burned low and only
one lamp was lit. His drawing-room had never
looked so cheerless. Nelly must be upstairs,
of course. How tiresome! Perhaps, though,
she had taken his displeasure to heart and
was really unwell. Poor dear! She certainly
seemed fond of him, he would go to her room
and make it all right without delay! Once,
twice he tapped at the door. No answer. So
he opened it without ceremony, and walked in.
Here, too, the fire was low and the room nearly
dark, but he could make out that it was
unoccupied. More, an empty wardrobe stood
open, and though several trinkets remained on
the dressing-table, Nelly's ivory hair-brushes,
with her monogram, his own gift, were gone.

He turned sick at heart, though he told
himself there was no cause for discomposure ;
but he ran downstairs again, nimbly enough,
to ring the drawing-room bell with considerable
violence.

The butler had gone to dress, and it was
answered by a footman.

"Where is Mrs. Roy?" he asked, trying
to speak in his ordinary voice.

"Mrs. Roy, sir? Mrs. Roy is gone, sir."

"Gone! What do you mean? Gone
where?"

The man looked surprised. "Mrs. Roy
ordered the carriage at half-past two, sir. It
took her to the station, and I understand she
went to London by the afternoon train."

He fairly gasped. But in whatever attitude
he goes down, a man is bound to fall decently,
like Julius Cæsar, before his own household ;
so he muttered something incoherent about
"bad news," and "he thought she would have
waited for a later train," but his manner was
sorely troubled, his voice came thick and

indistinct. The footman retired calmly, less concerned than might be supposed. I imagine our domestics are not easily affected by such symptoms of mental disorder. Judging from analogy, they account for them in the charitable supposition that "Master is a little the worse for drink."

Put him face to face with an emergency, John Roy had courage and presence of mind enough. Both were now supplemented by a strong sense of indignation and ill-usage.

"Gone to London by the afternoon train!" he muttered, walking up and down his deserted drawing-room in momentary expectation that dinner would be announced. "Of course! I see it all! And that scoundrel, too. They were found out too soon, and she did not dare face me again. But *he* shall, and pretty close too, if we have to travel a thousand miles for it. Steady now! I must look at this business as if I were acting for some one else. The first point is to avoid anything like a show-up before the servants. I can do nothing to-morrow till the post comes in, then I shall go to London by the twelve o'clock train, and find a friend at once. Who is there I can ask to see me through such a three-cornered business —for I mean to shoot Fitzowen as sure as he stands there?"

This was a knotty problem, involving some consideration. He had not settled it when he went to dinner, and resolved during the progress of that ceremony, which he sat through with praiseworthy endurance, to decide nothing till he had visited his club, and seen which of his old friends were in town.

But with all his anger, all his resolution, there were moments during that long cheerless evening when his heart smote him sore. The image of Nelly would pass before him, as he used to watch her moving about the very room in which he sat, busy with some little arrangement for his comfort and convenience, or, dearer still, as he remembered her at Beachmouth during that brief courtship, when she had seemed to him a very paragon of womankind, no less for beauty of character and person than for the adoration she lavished on himself.

Of all blessings, a wife is, perhaps, that of which a man becomes most sensible in its loss. John Roy could not help suspecting that he had not himself been entirely without blame ; that a little patience, a little consideration, a little forbearance might have preserved to him the affections of her fond and gentle nature, true and tender as when they watched the sea-gulls together on the southern coast, and thought nothing could ever come between them this side the grave.

CHAPTER XVII.

BAFFLED.

FOR one who has ever lived long enough in London to make it a home, there is something in the stir and bustle of its streets, the shifting variety of its faces, the very tread of busy feet on its pavement, that brings his mind, as it were, to its proper bearings, causing him to appraise himself, his affairs, and his interests at their real value, and reminding him that any one individual, though the centre of his own circle, is but an insignificant unit in the great scheme.

Before John Roy had rattled through half-a-dozen streets, and shaved as many lamp-posts, in a hansom cab, he began to take a clearer view of his position, and to suspect that he might have been in a greater hurry than

behoved a man of his experience, who had seen
so much of life. It was unwise thus to jump,
without inquiry, to conclusions. It would
have been better to put his pride in his pocket,
and get what information he could from the
railway officials at his own station concerning
his wife and her supposed travelling-companion,
before he rushed up to London, breathing blood
and gunpowder, on an expedition that might
turn out a fool's-errand after all!

Such reflections came too late. He had
arrived in town by the early train for a
particular purpose, and he must carry it
through. Obviously, the first thing to be
done was to dress at an hotel and go down at
once to his club.

Yet, for all his knowledge of the world, it
seemed strange to this man, whose mind was
preoccupied with matters of life and death,
that half-a-dozen acquaintances whom he had
not seen for years should greet him, as if they
were in the habit of meeting every day, with
a careless nod and a growl at the east wind.

Truly, your London welcome is the reverse of gushing, and an earthquake would hardly affect the well-bred placidity of St. James's Street if it took place east of Temple Bar.

Club usages and club manners are of themselves. In other phases of life men may seem pleased with the society of their friends, and even interested in their welfare; but as soon as they have passed the hall-porter and received their letters, such exuberance of natural feeling is at once discarded. As a huntsman puts on his kennel-coat when he goes amongst his hounds, so the members of these social institutions think well to clothe themselves from head to foot in an indifference which, but for its exceeding carelessness, would not be far removed from disgust.

Like most reserved people, John Roy was somewhat impressionable. It is not too much to say that he felt both discouraged and disheartened as, entering the morning-room of the Junior Amalgamated, he scanned nervously the array of hats and newspapers representing the members of that exclusive association. Where all faces were hidden it was difficult to identify a friend, and his spirit sank, while he reflected how severely he must put that friend's attachment to the test. Shy, awkward, and perplexed, he walked stiffly to the fire-place, feeling, like a thorough Englishman, that his present ordeal was the most unpleasant part of the whole business. A true Briton stands fire better than inspection, quailing pitifully before a battery that consists of impassible faces and calm, inquiring eyes.

On the hearth-rug he brushed against a gentleman in an easy-chair, completely hidden behind the broad sheet of the *Times*. Turning to apologise, he found himself face to face, of all people in the world, with Lord Fitzowen.

It would feebly express John Roy's discomfiture to say you might have knocked him down with a feather. He stood with his mouth open in dumb surprise.

The other nodded, yawned, rose and stretched himself.

"How d'ye do, Roy?" said he. "Why didn't you come up yesterday with me and St. George there? I found him at the station. I suppose you won't go away again now. Have you brought Mrs. Roy?"

No man could put on this assumption of complete innocence had he been the cleverest actor that ever wore paint: besides, "St. George there," who was in the room, could have attested the veracity of Fitzowen's statement, and John Roy felt utterly at a loss. There was nothing for it but to regain his composure as best he might, and shake by the hand the man he had meant to shoot through the head, with such overdone cordiality as should serve to cover his own confusion.

"It's only a flying visit," he stammered. "Business and that kind of thing. Going down again this evening. Town rather empty still. Nothing to keep one here just now."

"Nonsense! Stay till to-morrow. Dine with me quietly—*en garçon*. Nobody but St. George. I've a box at the Deucalion.

We'll see the 'Ugly Duck.' It's rather a good burlesque, and bring What's-her-name back to supper. It wouldn't be bad fun."

Such evidence being circumstantial, and therefore of the best kind, became more conclusive with every word. It was beyond all bounds of probability that a gentleman who had run away with his friend's wife less than twenty-four hours ago, should be entertaining bachelors at dinner, asking actresses to supper, and otherwise partaking of those amusements on which feminine influence of any kind puts an immediate extinguisher; nor was it credible that he should calmly invite the injured husband to participate in such demonstrations of independence and self-government at a moment's notice, without any hesitation or embarrassment whatsoever. Again John Roy excused himself, though in his heart half tempted to accept, so completely had the atmosphere of London changed his sentiments in the space of two hours.

"I see," said Fitz, laughing good-humouredly; "Mrs. Roy won't stand it! Quite right. Give her my kind regards. After all, you have the best of it. There is something very superior and respectable in being a married man!"

With whomsoever Nelly had run away, the culprit was clearly not Lord Fitzowen.

John Roy walked out of the Junior Amalgamated a good deal easier of mind than he walked in; yet, strange to say, conscious that his displeasure against his wife was stronger now than while he believed her criminal conduct had estranged her from him for ever. She seemed a belligerent then, declaring open war, now she was only a vassal who had rebelled.

Turning matters over in his mind, he made sure she had taken refuge with her aunt. He would go to Corner Street at once, and bring her back, but in such a manner as to make her feel the whole weight of his dissatisfaction, and prevent her from ever having recourse to such refractory measures again.

He was soon at the Corner Hotel: it had never appeared so close, dirty, and uncomfortable before. Again came over him the unworthy feeling that he had descended too low in his choice, and that from the very beginning his marriage was a mistake.

This untoward mood seemed only aggravated by his reception. Mrs. Phipps, in the dingiest of caps, no sooner heard his name than she rushed at him open-armed, then curtsied and looked foolish, seeing that he eluded her embrace.

This good lady's face was browner and more oblong than ever, her dress more faded, her forehead more shiny, her general appearance, he thought, had changed sadly for the worse.

"Why you're quite a stranger, Mr. Roy," she exclaimed: "now do set down and rest yourself. You'll take a glass of wine, I hope. But first and foremost, how's Nelly? You've brought her with you, in course?"

He was taken aback, and looked it.

"Nelly!" he repeated. "Is she not with *you*? I came here to look for her."

Mrs. Phipps dropped into an arm-chair with a plump that spoke volumes for her confidence in its strength.

"You come here to look for her!" she gasped. "Oh, Mr. Roy, whatever do you mean?"

He was vexed beyond measure. "Mrs. Roy has chosen to leave her home, madam," he answered harshly, "and were she not dead to all proper feeling she would have come straight here. Had I found her under your protection, I might have been prevailed upon to look over such conduct in consideration of promised amendment for the future. But she has taken her own line, and I shall now feel justified in taking mine."

"Mr. Roy, you drove her to it!"

"I have no wish to exchange recriminations, Mrs. Phipps. If you choose to support your niece in her outrageous defiance of all social laws, of the customs, even the decencies of

life, that is your affair. I shall decline to
communicate with either of you, except through
a solicitor."

"You drove her to it, Mr. Roy! If it was
my last breath, I'd say it. When she left this
house to get married—and a black day it
seems to have been—there wasn't a better
behaved young woman in all London than
Nelly, nor a better principled, nor a better
brought-up. There may be faults on both
sides. I'm not a-going to say as there isn't.
But when you come to leaving a home like
yours, and going out alone into the wide
world, nobody shall persuade me but what
I told you before is gospel truth, and you
drove her to it, Mr. Roy. You did, as sure as
you stand there!"

Mrs. Phipps, who loved her niece, seemed a
thorough woman, insensible to argument, but
staunch in her affections. It was no use
disputing the point, and John Roy was forced
to content himself with as dignified a retreat
as could be made under the circumstances, for

his hostess followed him, even to the street-door, with a volley of reproaches that gathered violence and incoherence at each successive discharge. The storm no doubt was succeeded by a torrent of tears, and the poor woman herself, in the midst of her dismay and anxiety, regretted bitterly that she had "spoke up," as she called it, with so much freedom, but her visitor had placed a quarter of a mile between them before this inevitable reaction, and it was too late to call him back.

He felt sadly perplexed. Nelly was gone, there could be no doubt, but where? If she had fled with Lord Fitzowen, he would have known how to act. If she had taken sanctuary in her aunt's hotel, he could have extricated her from that unsavoury refuge, with a certain loss of dignity, perhaps, but an undoubted accession of authority for the future. In either case his course would have been clear. But now she had baffled him completely. How could he return to Royston Grange without his wife? How reply to the inquiries of a whole neighbourhood that she had gone away from him, he didn't know where? He must have time for consideration. He ought not to be in a hurry. To-morrow or next day something might turn up. He had better stop in London, he thought, wishing heartily that he had never left it.

CHAPTER XVIII.

DO YOU REMEMBER?

WHAT should he do with himself in the mean time? He looked at his watch. It was a little after four. The Academy had not yet opened, Hurlingham was too far off, Prince's was sure to be empty at this hour, and with the thermometer scarcely ten degrees above freezing, nobody would be in the Park. There was still a long blank to fill up before the earliest possible dinner, and the only choice of pastime lay between a visit to Christie and Manson's and a Turkish bath.

He had almost decided in favour of the latter, when a Victoria pulled up with a jerk so close to the kerbstone, that its stiff leathern wing brushed his elbow, while a lady bent on shopping, and enveloped in furs, landed on the pavement under his very nose.

"Good gracious, Mr. Roy!" exclaimed a voice that had haunted him for many a weary day since he heard it last, that he had not quite forgotten even now. "Is it you or your ghost? What ages since we met? I can't say how glad I am to see you again!"

It was Lady Jane, and nobody else! The Lady Jane of whom he had taken leave long years ago, under the elms in Kensington Gardens, with a few hurried words of sorrowing kindness and good-will, sorely curtailed because of that matron's proximity to whom Jane had been temporarily intrusted, and who "stood in" with the lovers, but only to a limited extent.

Now, the one was a prosperous widow, already out of black, the other, a husband, whom we may term unattached, smarting under a sense of conjugal ill-usage, and disposed to separate himself conclusively from his wife.

Lady Jane could not but feel gratified by
the confusion of his manner while he returned
her greeting.   Though a woman's empire have
been swept away ever so completely, she likes
to think that its glories are not wholly forgotten.
What is it all but a dream? an illusion of
which, perhaps, memory is the sweetest and
most substantial charm!

"I—I hope you're quite well," stammered
the gentleman, "I didn't know you were in
town."

"How should you?" she answered kindly,
and with perfect self-possession. "It is a
century since you and I have forgotten each
other, or—tried to, at any rate."

The last very faintly, and with a downward
look that used to be most effective. "When
at close quarters, aim low!" was her maxim,
and Lady Jane's fire could do execution
still.

"Do not say forgotten," he replied, trying
to recover himself, as behoved a man-of-the-
world. "It's not so very long, after all, and

to look at *you* it seems as if we had been walking together only last week!"

"You always used to flatter one," she answered coquettishly. "Now, will you come and see me? Don't say no, for the sake of old times."

"When?"

"Any day. To-day, if you like. I am always in at five. I am on my way home now. Twenty-seven in the next street. I shall expect you in a quarter of an hour."

There were but a few minutes to talk, and they passed quickly enough. He walked like a man in a dream. He felt as if his Mexican life, his return home, his vegetation at Royston Grange, even his marriage to Miss Burton, were fancies of the sleeper that had disappeared with morning light. Yes, he was awake now; and nothing seemed real but Lady Jane.

Very real, too, and more substantial than of old. Face and figure were both rounder and fuller than when last they parted, all those years ago; but, like many English beauties, his first love's maturity was handsomer than her girlhood, and, had it been otherwise, what matter? The charm was in her eyes and voice still, it woke up feelings that had only slept while he believed them dead. John Roy began to think that, without knowing it, he might have been in love with two women at once all the time.

"Lady Jane at home?"

"Yes, sir," and mounting a dark staircase, pervaded by a heavy odour of hot-house plants, he found himself bowing over her ladyship's white hand, with more of deference and even devotion than is absolutely essential to politeness in a mere morning call.

But he began to talk about the weather nevertheless, forgetting, in his perturbation, that when conversing with a lady, it is only good manners, and saves a deal of trouble besides, to let her "make the running" from end to end.

She wasted little of her energies on the east

wind. Before his tea was cool enough to drink, she asked him pointedly whether he found her much altered, and wondered that he recognised her at once!

"I should have known you anywhere," he answered. "Do you think I forget so easily?"

The cream-jug in her hand shook a little, perhaps by accident.

"What is all one's life," she returned, "but trying to forget? It's the lesson everybody has to learn. I fancy it comes harder to women then men."

"You succeeded pretty easily. You didn't want much teaching, perhaps you've a natural talent independent of education."

"Why do you say that? It's unkind. If I wanted to be rude, I should say, it's untrue. How can you tell what I have thought, or not thought, done, or not done, since—since we both were young and foolish. You've not taken much trouble to find out."

She had ingeniously turned the tables, and put him on his defence. He looked foolish, and replied vaguely, " did you ever expect to see me again ? "

" No. But I *hoped* it ? "

" Lady Jane, were you *really* glad to meet me ? Do you mean that you still—that you still—— "

" Let me give you some more tea. No ? Well, sit down again, don't go away yet. I want you to tell me all about your wife."

His face fell, and he fidgeted in his chair. With a woman's tact she saw there was something wrong, and continued in the same easy confidential tone—

" I was pleased—yes—I think I was *really* pleased to hear of your marriage. I had a great mind to write and congratulate you."

" Why didn't you ? "

" Well, there were reasons. If my poor husband had been alive, I should have done it frankly enough. Matrimony is the best and happiest state for people, after all."

" I am glad you found it so. It is not everybody's experience. I am rather of Dr.

Johnson's opinion, that marriages would turn out better if they were arranged by the Lord Chancellor."

"Mine *was*. At least we could do nothing without his consent. My poor husband did not come of age till he was five-and-twenty. It made a great many complications, and at one time I very nearly changed my mind."

"But it answered? You were happy together, I suppose?"

"We got on very well. Yes—I can't say it answered badly. He did everything I told —I mean, I asked him. Still, Mr. Roy, when people are to pass their whole lives together, it's a fearful risk. However little one expects, one is sure to be disappointed."

"But you married a man in your own station; that is a great point. You never could have borne with somebody you were ashamed of. Mr. de Banier came of a very old family, I believe?"

"Very. But—but his father was in trade all the same. No; I shouldn't say the de

Baniers were exactly in our own set. Do you think that matters so much?"

" I think it is the most important consideration of all."

" What? More important than that people should like each other? You used not to be so practical. Do you remember our argument on that very subject at Lady Yorkminster's ball?"

" Do *you*?"

" Every word of it. I could tell you the very names of the couples that passed us on their way to the tea-room. I could tell you the number of the dance we sat out. I believe I've got my card still. You had a white flower in your button-hole, and I wondered whether it was given you by my cousin Blanche."

" What a memory you have. Is it of the head, or the heart?"

" Nonsense. Tell me about yourself. When did you come to town? Where are you staying? I am dying to know Mrs. Roy."

He hesitated; but she looked so kind, so

sympathising, and withal so handsome, that he took the plunge.

"Lady Jane," said he, "I don't mind your knowing the truth. The fact is we—we—don't get on very well together, and Mrs. Roy is not with me at present."

She tried to seem sorrowful and commiserating, but there was a latent sparkle in her blue eyes, a something of satisfaction in her tone, while she answered, "I am so grieved to hear it. Don't you think, Mr. Roy, if you tried patience and kindness, she might be brought to reason? I can't understand anybody quarrelling with *you!*"

There is an *esprit de corps* in the sex which prompts every woman ostensibly to stand up for another. It takes but little persuasion, however, to satisfy her that the erring sister is wholly in the wrong.

"I have my faults," he answered, "but I don't think I am inclined to be hasty or unreasonable. Lady Jane, I will trust you entirely, and I feel sure you will not abuse my confidence. In the first place, were you surprised to hear of my marriage?"

"A little. I thought—I thought—Never mind what I thought."

"Well, it seems to be one's fate to make some great mistake in life sooner or later. I wonder whether the lady I chose, was the least the sort of person you would have expected me to marry. I did a foolish thing, and now I have to pay for it."

Sympathy and curiosity, two very strong motives, prompted her ladyship to discharge a volley of inquiries, but she possessed a large share of that discretion which is only acquired in the uninterrupted training of society, and contented herself with a kindly glance and a sigh of commiseration.

"My wife," he continued, "though well-born and well-educated, is not—is not exactly one of the people you are accustomed to meet. In short, she don't quite understand the ways of society. You see, she has never lived much in the great world."

"Has she been presented at Court?" interrupted Lady Jane earnestly. "That is where the line should always be drawn. I heard she had *not.*"

"Then you *did* hear about my marriage?"

"Of course. I was interested, and I asked. Can you wonder?"

"I never wonder. Still, there is such a thing as an agreeable surprise. I thought I had passed out of your life, and that even my name never came into your head."

"You thought nothing of the kind. Do you suppose a woman gives up her—her friendships in that way, even under the hardest pressure, without scruple or regret? How little you understand us! Well, well—that's over and done with now! Let me hear all about it, Mr. Roy. Were you *very* much in love?"

"With Lady Jane? Yes; I am sure I told her so often enough."

"And she believed you. One need not be ashamed of the truth now. But you understand what I mean. Were you very much in love with your wife when you proposed to her—let me see, only the end of last summer? or was it one of those scrapes men get into from sheer laziness, and want of moral courage to say, No?"

He had chivalry enough to scorn the loophole she left for his escape.

"Yes, I *was* in love with her," he answered rather sadly. "I thought she would have made me happy. Never mind, I can do without her. I dare say it's all for the best."

"Poor Mr. Roy!" murmured her ladyship, "I am sorry. You know I am, don't you?"

"I know you have a kind and sympathising nature, Lady Jane," he answered, putting on his gloves as with intention of presently taking leave; "that is why I am inflicting my troubles on you now. It's not a long story, and I will begin at the beginning. Last summer I went to Beachmouth, simply because I was bored at home, meaning to have a dip in the sea, spend

Sunday, and go back. Lady Jane, I stayed there three weeks."

"You found the Sundays so amusing, I conclude."

"Every day was a holiday. Each seemed brighter than the last. I never was so happy in my life. Never—but once."

"I am not going to ask you when that was. Go on."

"The very first evening I was struck by the appearance of a lady staying at the hotel; and next day, through the merest accident, I succeeded in making her acquaintance. I found her frank, pleasant, unaffected, and handsomer even than I thought."

"Dark or fair?"

"Dark, with beautiful black hair."

"How odd; you never used to admire dark women. Well, how long did this seaside romance go on before—excuse me, Mr. Roy—before you made a fool of yourself?"

"Not long. We met half-a-dozen times a day. I thought she seemed to like me, and soon hardened my heart to ask whether she really did or not. Then she told me all about herself, making no secret of her birth and bringing up. Her father was a bookseller, and her aunt kept an hotel."

"Mr. Roy, how could you?"

"I *could* and I *did.* We were married in London, and I carried her off to Royston Grange, firmly persuaded that with a few hints, and a little practice among our country neighbours, she would make as good a lady as if she had been registered in the Stud-book—I beg your pardon; I mean the Peerage."

"They never do. You see it didn't answer."

"That was no fault of mine. I took the greatest pains—explained everything, rehearsed everything. She wasn't obstinate, she wasn't exactly stupid; but somehow she seemed unable to take it in. After a time she lost her spirits, grew pale and silent; but declared there was nothing the matter, even while she looked up from her work with eyes full of tears."

"Poor thing! Perhaps she was unhappy."

"She *was* unhappy, Lady Jane, but not about *me*. Yesterday, at a moment's notice, she left her home during my absence, as far as I can learn, without a companion of any kind."

Lady Jane pondered. "Have you reason to suspect that she—that she cares for anybody in particular?"

"I had, and now I have *not*. I am puzzled —I am at my wits' end. She left no letter, no message. I am not even sure that she is in London. A man can't well advertise for his wife—can't have her cried like a lost dog. Lady Jane, what would you advise me to do?"

"Nothing!" answered her ladyship with decision. "That is always safe. Go about among your friends—show yourself everywhere. If people ask after Mrs. Roy, say you have come up to take a house, and she is to join you in London. Then they will insist on their own favourite· situation, and that changes the subject. In the mean time confide in nobody but me. You may be sure I have your welfare at heart. When shall I see you again? Come and dine here to-morrow. My sister is in town; I'll ask her to meet you, and we will go to the French Play. Good-bye, Mr. Roy, but not for quite so long as last time. To-morrow, at half-past seven. Don't forget."

He bent over the hand she gave him till his lips almost touched her rings, and walked down-stairs, thinking the world a much better place to live in than it seemed an hour or two ago.

CHAPTER XIX.

IN THE WILDERNESS.

LIKE Hagar in her banishment, Nelly felt utterly desolate and forlorn when she turned her back on the home that had once seemed such a paradise, in which but a few weeks ago she had promised herself long years of wedded happiness and love. Like Hagar, too, she was faint and weary from physical exhaustion. Mr. Roy's displeasure had taken away her appetite for breakfast, and she forgot all about luncheon, though it was ready on the table when she went away. It cost her a painful effort to preserve composure before the servants at the hall-door, and she parried with difficulty the curiosity of her maid, who could not understand why Mrs. Roy had packed a trunk with her own hands, or how that lady could possibly dispense with her ministrations for a single night.

At the station, too, where she arrived long before the train, her footman seemed exceedingly loth to be dismissed with the carriage as ordered, and proposed, though hardly in good faith, to return on foot the whole way, rather than not see Mrs. Roy's luggage into the guard's van with his own eyes. When these objections had been overruled, and the trot of the dear horses died out on the far high road, our outcast felt very forlorn indeed. Behind her was the still fondly beloved patriarch on whom she could not bear to think; before her a future too vague and gloomy to contemplate; while about her brooded the desolate silence of an unfrequented railway station.

Poor Hagar turned into the ladies' waiting-room to cry. No doubt it did her good, but looking in the glass over the fireplace, she could not but observe that her eyes were swollen and her nose was red.

Presently a spectral arm, shot out from the

signal-post, denoted the arrival of her train.
It was time to emerge and take a ticket. She
shrank back to her hiding-place, nevertheless,
in considerable vexation and dismay when she
caught sight of Lord Fitzowen on the platform,
laughing and talking with a young man of his
own age, in dress, manners, and appearance an
exact counterpart of himself.

"Of all people on earth," thought Nelly,
"this is the last I wanted to meet. How can
I explain to him why I am here and where I
am going? Besides, I look perfectly hideous.
He is sure to see I have been crying. Good
gracious! If he was to ask me the reason, and
I couldn't keep from bursting out again!
What would his friend think? What would
he think himself? No. Here I shall stay till
I've seen them safe off. After all that has
passed, rather than travel by the same train
with Lord Fitzowen, perhaps in the same
carriage, I would never go near London
again!"

So she flattened her face against the

window, and watched the two gentlemen into a first-class compartment labelled "Smoking" with eager eyes and a beating heart, waiting impatiently enough, till the train panted on, and disappeared.

Then she drank some water from a dusty caraffe, sat down, and collected her energies to think out the whole situation. Once, in momentary weakness, she half resolved to walk back on foot to Royston Grange, and be reconciled with its master; but her heart was still too sore, and she dismissed the idea almost as soon as it arose.

Consulting a time-table, aided by a sympathising railway porter, she made up her mind to go down the line to a certain junction some thirty miles distant, where she could meet a late express, that, from inability to keep its time, was called, in contumely, The Flying Dutchman, and so proceeding to London arrive there in the middle of the night; but this intricate plan of operations she was unable to carry out. At the hour when she should have been taking her seat in The Dutchman she was in bed at an hotel, where she had resorted to get some tea, with a headache that incapacitated her from standing or even sitting upright.

"What does it matter?" thought poor Nelly. "Nobody expects me; nobody cares if I am alive or dead! Auntie has got accustomed to do without me, and nothing would please Mr. Roy better than to be quite sure he would never hear of me again."

She did them both injustice. Mr. Roy was seeking her in London before her headache allowed her to get out of bed; and when, on the second day after her departure from Royston Grange, she arrived at the Corner Hotel, it needed but one look in her relative's face to be assured of Auntie's overpowering anxiety and her delight at the wanderer's return.

"So he came *here* to find me?" repeated Nelly for the twentieth time, when she had taken her bonnet off and settled down in her

own old place. "Did he look disappointed?
Did he seem sorry, Auntie, or what?"

"Sorry?" returned Mrs. Phipps—a practical
person, who called spades and everything else
by their right names. "Not a bit! Angry,
if you like. There was a precious blow-up! I
can tell you. I gave him a piece of my mind,
and he went away in a huff."

"He'll come again," said Nelly. "He
must, if he's in earnest. Don't you think,
Auntie, he is sure to come again?"

"I hope not," replied her aunt. "You're
better without him, my dear. I never thought
much of them consequential, stuck-up ways of
his. When he made you a lady, why didn't
he treat you as such? No, no, you're better
without him, Nelly, depend upon it. You've
got a comfortable home here as long as you
like to stay, and for my part I hope he will
never darken our doors again."

Nelly did not quite agree, yet she often
asked herself how she would decide if her
husband were to propose that she should come

back and live with him once more. Hurt,
vexed, humiliated, she could yet have forgiven
him only too readily; but, because she loved
him so dearly, it seemed better that she should
never see him again. As the nightingale is
said to lean her breast against a thorn; as the
horse, most assuredly, in his gallant, generous
nature, presses down and crouches on the stake
that drains his life-blood away, so does woman
seem to derive some mysterious and morbid
gratification while hugging her keenest sorrows
tight to her bosom, and immolating herself at
the altar of an unworthy idol, that looks down
on the sacrifice calm, pitiless, and imperturbable,
with a stony smile. But whatever might have
been her decision, she would have liked at
least the option of refusing. And day by day
Nelly's step became heavier, the colour faded
from her cheek, as visitor after visitor poured
into the hotel, but no Mr. Roy.

He was differently employed. Putting off,
from week to week, his intention of going back, he left Mrs. Mopus, much to her

contentment, in sole command at Royston
Grange, while he amused himself with the
gaieties of early spring in London, and devoted
his spare time to the dangerous society of Lady
Jane.

It was not long before people began to talk.
" So sorry we could not come to you, my dear,
we dined with Lady Jane de Banier. Who
had you? Mr. Roy, of course! It's really
getting too barefaced. She has not been a
widow eighteen months, and there she is,
flaunting about in colours, and I don't know
what all, with a married man! It's true, my
dear, I assure you. There's a wife hidden
away somewhere in the country. Lord Fitzowen has seen her, and declares she is perfectly
beautiful. Jane ought really to be spoken to.
One *must* draw a line; and if nobody else
has courage to give her a hint, I will do it
myself?"

So Jane *was* spoken to, with the usual
result. She resented such interference warmly,
and became only the more engrossed with her

present fancy, that it was represented as injurious to the future of her children, and hazardous to her own good name. "I suppose you would have me go about in a *yash-mak*, with a guard of what-do-you-call-'ems," protested her ladyship, tossing her head in high dudgeon. "Thank you, I'd rather not! I am a Christian woman in a Christian country, and I think I am the best judge of my own conduct."

Then she had a quiet little cry, and sat down to write an incoherent note to Mr. Roy, entreating him not to come near her again, which brought him to her door in a violent hurry within half an hour of its delivery.

It must be admitted, however, that although her friends expressed great dissatisfaction among themselves, they dined with her readily enough, notwithstanding the obnoxious Mr. Roy, issuing their own invitations to the imprudent couple freely in return, so as to afford them every opportunity of meeting at home and abroad.

Ere long the one was never asked to anything without the other, and an easy-going world made up its mind to recognise this indiscreet renewal of former intimacy as "an established thing."

Society has compiled a code of its own for which it is answerable to itself, and has ruled that "one person may steal a horse while another must not look at a halter." The principle is sufficiently elastic, and it has been so liberally extended of late that the horse-stealers are increasing every day. I do not mean to infer Lady Jane was one of these. Her conduct, though imprudent, originated in the only natural and healthy impulse of her artificial life. In girlhood she had liked John Roy honestly enough—had loved him, indeed, in so far as she was capable of that unworldly sentiment. She gave him up perhaps too readily, but who knows what amount of pressure was put on her in her own family? The female department has its secrets in the households of Mayfair as of Stamboul. I dare

say she often lay awake crying, and envied the
sweeps or the milkman when her mamma
thought she was sound asleep. I dare say,
while she stood at the altar in that love of a
wedding dress (*corsage Louis Quatorze*), she
glanced approvingly at her bridegroom, who
was as spruce as a new pin, and admitted that
she liked him better than anybody in the
world—" bar one ! "

So she made Mr. de Banier a good wife
enough, managing his house, ordering his
dinner, and contradicting him no more than
was absolutely necessary before his servants or
his guests. She nursed him, too, kindly and
tenderly through his last illness, and, perhaps,
never felt so attached to him in her life, as the
day the doctor gave him over.

For weeks after the funeral she refused to
see a soul, going softly about the house with a
pale face and red eyes; so that the very maids
declared they " never thought her ladyship had
been one to take on like that ! " And she put
up a monument to his memory, unequalled in

hideousness, that cost the best part of a thousand pounds.

When she found herself a rich widow, still handsome, in the prime of life, was she to be wholly debarred from those pleasures of the heart, she had given up so dutifully to obey papa and mamma? Lady Jane thought not. She saw men in society every day on whom she might have set her affections with the certainty of a return; but she had always been fastidious, and now seemed more than ever hard to please. This one was vulgar, the other overbearing, a third hunted, a fourth smoked, and the vacant situation had not yet been filled on the afternoon when she went out shopping in her Victoria, and met Mr. Roy.

She experienced a want in life, which the society of her children—two slips of girls and a fat-headed little boy—proved quite inadequate to supply. There are women for whom the interests of a nursery can be the end and aim of existence; but Lady Jane, though a kind, even an indulgent mother, was not one of these. She had dreamed her dreams, as the most practical of us will; had even imagined an ideal of her own, an impossible person, full of antagonistic qualities, good and bad; which misty phantom she dressed in the remnants of her old, worn-out attachment, and believed that it reminded her of Mr. Roy—was it likely that she should let him go, when he came once more within range of her attractions,—a lonely man, ill-used, disappointed, with a history, and, perhaps, none the less desirable that he hung just out of reach, and was not exactly free.

I am little surprised, for one, that she should have asked him to tea, and then to dinner, and afterwards to come and see her whenever he liked. Finally, that she made her servants understand she was always at home to Mr. Roy, and to nobody else when he called.

"Love is of man's life a thing apart," says Byron. I fear that with the ruder and less sensitive half of our species, this delightful fallacy requires certain favourable conditions, both of body and mind, to become the one engrossing occupation of both. Love-in-idleness, however, is a plant that needs but little care or culture to arrive at rich maturity. Like the young trees of the thrifty Scotsman, it is growing while we are sleeping; and a man who has nothing to do finds plenty of time for folly when the occasion offers.

John Roy, neglecting his duties as a country gentleman and landowner, living vaguely from hand to mouth, as it were, at a London hotel, undecided how to act, with no certain task for to-day, no definite intentions for to-morrow, was of all people in the world the most likely to drift into some egregious absurdity, from a mere sense of helplessness and discouragement, a morbid conviction that it was impossible for him to keep straight, and even if he did, by painful self-denial, succeed in following the right road after all, what was the good!

But he was by no means happy; his self-love had been grievously wounded; and Lady

Jane's continued preference, however flattering, could not heal the sore. It was pleasant, no doubt, and not very expensive, to send her bouquets, and paper-cutters, and stalls at the French Play. He experienced a certain excitement in watching for her appearance at a party, in catching her eye across a room, with the consciousness that there was a something between them in which the bystanders had no share; and in putting her affectionately into her carriage when she went away. Still there was also a sense of sameness about the whole affair, he was going over the old ground that had been traversed often enough before; and a path even of roses may become wearisome when it has to be trodden again and again. We catch ourselves saying precisely the same things to Mary that we said to Jane; Susan's pressure of the hand is exactly like poor Henrietta's; and how can we send cut flowers to Margaret without repeating the message that used to be forwarded with her posies to Kate? Sometimes he admitted that, even if he *had* married Lady Jane, he might have got tired of her. Did he ever feel tired of Nelly? No! A thousand times no! Annoyed, irritated, provoked, fancying he wished he had never seen her; but weary of her? Certainly not. In his married life there had been nothing irksome, nothing out of character, nothing of that continued sense of effort which is so exhausting to a man in a false position, and which made him feel something akin to relief, rather than disappointment, on those rare occasions when he passed an afternoon without dancing attendance on Lady Jane.

How could he be happy while continually at war with himself? Now he would seek Nelly out, no matter where she was hiding, humble himself at her feet, and entreat her to return to a home that should never be entered but by their own two selves. Anon he resolved to take legal measures for a separation, nay, move heaven and earth for a divorce, that he might put an end to this unsatisfactory state of things by a marriage with Lady Jane. And still he lived on from day to day, settling nothing, doing nothing, alternately making and breaking resolutions of amendment, but calling, nevertheless, at No. 27 as persistently and nearly as often as the penny post.

CHAPTER XX.

A BLUE-JACKET.

IN the mean time Nelly settled down to her former habits at the Corner Hotel, much to the gain of that establishment in matters of cleanliness and comfort. Mrs. Phipps, who had missed her sadly, while protesting against her own selfishness, could not but rejoice to have her back, estimating at its real value her niece's supervision of a continually changing household. Mrs. Roy, who now chose to call herself Mrs. John, as a compromise between the assertion of a married woman's dignity and the independence of an *alias*, resumed without a murmur the old leathern stool on its three high legs, the folio volumes ruled in red ink, the long quills, the bunches of keys, and other appliances of that authority which was

exercised from her seat of government, a glass
cage off the entrance-hall, secluded from the
light of day.

Servants and tradespeople saw little difference in her demeanour. Punctual, exact,
methodical, always decided, while always
courteous, she might be graver in manner and
slower in gesture than of old, but that was
all. "Mrs. John had known trouble," they
observed, "along of a good-for-nothing 'usband."
Such a calamity, being in no way remarkable,
demanded little pity and less surprise. Only
her aunt looked below the surface. Mrs.
Phipps, vexed and saddened, told herself that
Nelly was breaking her heart for an unworthy
object, as she phrased it, "out of sheer
nonsensical trumpery and trash."

It was not long before the good woman
boiled over and spoke out.

"You'll do yourself a mischief, my dear,"
she expostulated, when, coming down to
breakfast earlier than usual one morning, she
found Nelly reading the Bible, bathed in tears.

"I wonder as you haven't more pride, I do. If it was me, I'd never so much as waste a thought on a man who could conduct himself like Mr. Roy, except to thank my stars I was well rid of him. I've no patience with you, nor him neither. A haughty, arbitrary, unfeeling, unprincipled Herod. That's what he is, and I wish he may be punished *like* Herod, and worse!"

"Why should you blame him, Auntie," answered Nelly, "if I don't? Didn't he come here after me, and couldn't I go back to him any moment if I chose? But I *don't* choose. It would only be misery for him and for me. Think what a dreadful thing for a man to be ashamed of his wife."

"Ashamed, Nelly! How can you speak so random? There's shame enough, I'll not deny it, but none on *our* side. In my opinion, the Archbishop of Canterbury, or the Queen, or the Lord Mayor, or somebody should have the power of undoing such a marriage as yours, just as if you had never been asked in church at all."

"Suppose I don't wish it undone?"

"Suppose the moon was made of green cheese! You ought to wish it, you ought to insist on it; and if I had to pay twenty lawyers, twenty times over, I'd spend my last shilling, but I'd see you righted. You've no spirit, Nelly, no more hadn't your poor mother. I only wish it was *me*. If they could keep me down like that, I'd let 'em."

"It's no use worrying, Auntie. People think so different. Why are both of us to be miserable? Surely one's enough. I dare say I expected too much. I have been disappointed, and must bear it the best I can. I've always got *you* left, and a happy home here, haven't I, as long as I like?"

"Happy home, indeed! Yes, it *was* a happy home before I let you go to that sinful place Beachmouth, and I wish the sea would rise to-night and wash clean over it, I do! Forgive and forget, says they, but I am one of them that can't forgive, and won't, even though I might forget. Nelly, Nelly, how can you look me in the face and mention the word *happy*, with your eyes as red as a chimney-sweep's, and all your beautiful colour gone?"

"Nobody is quite unhappy who is doing right, Auntie. I may be a little low, and out of spirits now, I don't deny it; but perhaps it's my own fault, thinking too much of things that cannot be helped. It will wear off after a time. Don't distress yourself about me. And, Auntie dear, if Mr. Roy *should* come and ask to see us, don't you fly in his face and be so short with him as you were last time, for my sake."

"Why, Nelly, you are not going to say you'd go back?"

"No, dear. I hardly think I should if he asked me ever so. But we won't speak of that. Who can tell what is going to happen, or where we may all be this day week? I don't care to look forward much. I'm quite content to stay as I am, only if you see me rather down sometimes don't you take notice. I'm such a silly that a word of kindness sets me off crying in a moment, and I can't stop."

"Crying, indeed!" concluded Mrs. Phipps. "I'd set some folks crying to a pretty tune if I had my way. There, Nelly, you could always coax your old aunt to do whatever you asked, from the time you was in short frocks. I'll say no more ; and if I could only see you look a little brighter, with a bit of colour in your cheek, there wouldn't be a happier woman than me between here and St. Paul's!"

So the good lady retired to the basement, where she could forget her vexation among those domestic implements she delighted to see in use ; while Nelly ruled another column in the ledger, and made out their week's bill for a family on the second floor, with unfailing accuracy of mind and finger, but with a heavy heart longing to be far away.

"Quite a superior person that Mrs. John," said the ostensible head of the family on the second floor to its actual ruler. "So quiet, so

ladylike, and—handsome, I should say, my
dear; shouldn't you?"

"I hardly looked at her," replied his wife,
whose feminine eye had scanned every feature
of Nelly's face, every article of her clothing,
with critical inspection. "Possibly she may
be attractive to people who admire that style.
I confess I cannot interest myself about a
barmaid!"

"Of course not, my dear," was the meek
rejoinder, equally sincere. "I only caught a
glimpse of her by accident. I dare say I was
mistaken. Can I do anything for you in the
Haymarket? I thought of going as far as the
Club."

Must I admit that he lingered in the
passage, asking for letters he had no reason to
expect, so as to have another look at Mrs. John,
if only through the blurred and dingy panes of
her glass cage?

Nor was this worthy gentleman, a roundabout person of mature age, under strict
control of his wife, the only visitor who

appreciated her attractions. Every stranger of
the male sex coming to engage rooms, whether
he went away disappointed or remained
rejoicing, paid his tribute of respectful tones
and admiring glances to the pale, sad, handsome woman who seemed to superintend this
establishment. Friends of Mrs. Phipps, suddenly remembering they had been shamefully
negligent, began to make afternoon calls with
increasing frequency, lingering and loitering in
hopes of being invited to tea, until some of the
more persistent discovered that the aunt
presided alone over this agreeable refreshment,
and the niece was satisfied with a solitary cup
and plate in her glass house. She kept them
at a distance all alike, and if not unconscious
of their admiration, accepted it with calm
disgust, as a necessary adjunct to the situation,
like blacks in a milk-jug or beetles on the
kitchen floor.

So the weeks dragged on. Easter set in, as
usual, with sleet and snow; the sweeps were
too cold to dance with any attempt at

merriment on May-day; and her Majesty's drawing-room was held in a pouring rain, that ladies clothed in virtue and loyalty, but otherwise most insufficiently clad, only hoped might be the forerunner of a thaw.

Everything seemed dismal enough. Tradesmen "supposed we should have a dull season," there was no news at the clubs, and those who make dinner-conversation asserted incredible statistics of houses to let, and coachmen out of place.

But people thronged into town, nevertheless. The authorities seized this opportunity to pick up the principal thoroughfares, so that London, in its main streets, became impassable for many hours of the day. Only by exercise of exceeding patience and dexterity, could the driver of a four-wheeled cab thread his way along the Strand, and when one of these vehicles stopped at the door of the Corner Hotel, Corner Street, the cabman grinned his thanks for an extra shilling, as having obeyed his fare's injunctions to "steer small."

Mrs. Phipps happened to meet this fresh arrival in the entrance. At the first glance she made a bounce that seemed to lift her a foot from the ground, and it is no reflection on her sense of propriety to affirm that she resisted with difficulty a strong impulse to fling her arms round his neck and hug him to her breast.

"What cheer, Mr. Brail?" she exclaimed, between laughing and crying, in the exuberance of her welcome. "What cheer? as you taught us to say before you sailed, and now I can't believe my eyes to see you back, and you looking so well and hearty, not a pin the worse!"

"The worse!" he repeated, taking both her hands; "why should I be the worse? Such a welcome as a man seems to get from all hands when he sets his foot on shore might bring him into port again though he had cleared out for the other world. England, home, and beauty, Mrs. Phipps—that's the ticket! *This* is home,

and *you* are beauty. Now can you give me
a bed?"

"Ah! you're the same man still! I'm sure
I wonder how you keep your head on without
somebody to hold it down! It wouldn't have
been *you*, of course, to have thought of writing
beforehand."

"I knew you would like a pleasant
surprise, my dear lady. I must have a bed
here in the old shop, and that's all about it!"

She looked affectionately in his frank, open
face, tanned by exposure to the colour of
mahogany, contrasting well with his short,
crisp, light-brown hair, bearing sailor written
on every line, and in thorough keeping with
his square, sinewy figure, his loose, powerful
limbs.

"I'm full," she said, "up to the attics. I
sent away a French family not an hour ago,
but I would rather turn out myself, and sleep
on the kitchen-dresser, than not make room
for *you*. Where is your luggage? your traps,

as you call them. Leave them there in the passage, while I go and ask Nelly what's to be done."

"Nelly! Miss Burton! Is she here still? Not spliced yet, nor *you* neither, Mrs. Phipps! That's even more extraordinary! If I'd known you were going to keep single for my sake, I would never have staid away all this time, cruising after the north pole!"

"Go along with you!" she answered, pushing him into her sitting-room. "You're no better than you always was, and you'll never mend your ways now; but bad as you are, I've lain awake many a stormy night thinking of you, and I am more than pleased, young man, I am humbly thankful to see you back at home once more!"

Collingwood Brail, Esq., Lieutenant in the Royal Navy, lately of her Majesty's ship *Aurora*, paid off after the Arctic Expedition, had frequented this Corner Street Hotel since the time when he used to run up from

Portsmouth on a week's leave, as mischievous
a midshipman as ever nibbled a biscuit, or cut
a brother reefer's hammock down by the head.
His frank boyish manners and kindly disposition wound themselves round the heart of
his landlady, who darned his stockings, mended
his shirts, and overhauled his kit generally on
so many occasions that she began to consider
him almost as a son. Once when, after a long
stare at the monument to Sir John Franklin
near the Duke of York's column, he found his
pocket picked of every shilling he possessed,
she insisted on keeping him till his leave
expired, without sending in her bill, and then
lent him a five-pound note to take him back to
his ship. She was fond of relating how, in
process of time, he returned the amount of his
debt in full, not forgetting gratuities to the
servants, by the hand of a staid messmate, who
did not conceal, perhaps, that the scraping of
such a sum together out of daily pay was
indeed, as young Brail described it, " a tight

fit." After he was "made" he wrote to her from the Tagus,—she had not an idea where it was, but prized her ship-letter all the more, producing it with great importance at tea-parties and such occasions of festivity, where it formed the principal topic of conversation.

' "It's not out of sight out of mind with the blue-jackets," she would say, wiping her eyes; "and the warmest hearts you will find in this world of ours, take my word for it, are the hearts of oak!"

' Many a time when a gale of wind swept over London, bringing showers of soot and dirt, with here and there a chimney-pot crashing into the street, her blood ran cold to realise the dangers her young sailor-friend must encounter ten thousand miles off, where, perhaps, he was pacing the deck impatient, in a dead calm, whistling for the breeze.

She could never be brought to understand this, entertaining a profound conviction that

day and night a seaman was always battling
for life, and regarded every member of the
profession as a hero and martyr, with a turn
for conviviality and light comedy, that ren-
dered him the pleasantest companion in the
world.

Next to her niece there was nobody for
whom she entertained so strong a personal
regard as Collingwood Brail.

And the man deserved it. Every inch of
him was gentleman and sailor—the finest
combination in the world. Plain and down-
right in conversation, but of a pleasant
good-nature that made it impossible to be
rude, he would differ with you frankly, but
never put you in the wrong; utterly devoid of
affectation in dress, manner, and sentiments,
he was scrupulously courteous and polite,
without yielding a jot of his own independence
or self-respect. Exceedingly deferential to
women, he did not seem to infer that they
belonged to a different order of beings either
above or below his own, and to offend one by

word or deed would have appeared to him no
less unmanly than to hurt a child. As in
person he was strong without being clumsy,
active without being restless; so, morally, he
possessed good sense without pomposity, and
courage without bravado.

Then, besides these solid qualities Mr. Brail
had a hundred trifling accomplishments, due to
his nautical training, invaluable in social life.
Nobody organised a pic-nic, even to the
tying-up of the hampers, with such facility and
such success. It seemed as if he could turn his
hand to anything, whether it were picketing
the horses, lighting a fire in the copsewood, or
washing plates and dishes when all was done,
and he had danced a hornpipe in and out the
crockery without damage to a single article.
In a country house, too, he was never late for
breakfast, never sleepy at night, dressed
quicker, and turned out neater, than any
dandy in the company; shot well if he was
asked, fished if they wanted him, rode to
hounds with unbounded nerve, if little judg-

ment, and under any conditions would have thought it as disgraceful to confess he was a pickpocket as to admit he was bored!

With the success he achieved in his own profession we have nothing to do, but it is easy to understand how such a character would be welcome everywhere to men, and exceedingly popular with women. When Mr. Brail paid one of his visits to Corner Street as a lieutenant of a year's standing, he found no difficulty in obtaining his share of those gaieties which are supposed to enliven the London season. It was at a flower-show in the Horticultural Gardens that our light-hearted sailor lost his liberty for good in a casual introduction to Miss Bruce. Never before had he found himself unequal to such social occasions, or utterly undone and consumed by a pair of bright eyes that only meant to enliven and to warm. It was all up with him in less than ten minutes. A handsome girl bending over the azaleas; a crafty old lady enjoying his discomfiture; an introduction; a bow; a walk to the next tent, and he was a free man no longer. To use his own words, "He hauled down his colours at the first shot, and for that kind of service never had the heart to hoist them again!"

END OF VOL. 1.